P9-DNE-805

secrets from the
Sleeping bag

Also by Rose Cooper

secrets from the
sleeping bag
A BLOGTASTIC! NOVEL BY
Rose Cooper
Delacorte Press

This is a work of fiction. Names, characters, places, and incidents either are the product of the author's imagination or are used fictitiously. Any resemblance to actual persons, living or dead, events, or locales is entirely coincidental.

 Published in the United States by Delacorte Press, an imprint of Random House Children's Books, a division of Random House, Inc., New York.

Delacorte Press is a registered trademark and the colophon is a trademark of Random House, Inc.

Visit us on the Web! randomhouse.com/kids

Educators and librarians, for a variety of teaching tools, visit us at randomhouse.com/teachers

Library of Congress Cataloging-in-Publication Data
Cooper, Rose.
Secrets from the sleeping bag : a blogtastic! novel / by Rose Cooper.
— 1st ed.
p. cm.
Summary: During four weeks of summer camp Sofia Becker writes all the juciest information in her notebook, so she can continue her blog when she returns home.
ISBN 978-0-385-74246-7 (hardcover) —
ISBN 978-0-375-99059-5 (lib. bdg.)
[1. Camps—Fiction. 2. Blogs—Fiction.] I. Title.
PZ7.C78768Sec 2012
[Fic]—dc23
2011046194

The text of this book is set in 12-point Providence-Sans.
Book design by Heather Daugherty

Printed in the United States of America
10 9 8 7 6 5 4 3 2 1

First Edition

Random House Children's Books supports the First Amendment and celebrates the right to read.

For my boys, Alexander and Samuel,

whom I love with all my heart,

and who have taught me that telling secrets

is much easier than keeping them.

ACKNOWLEDGMENTS

It's not a secret that the readers of *Blogtastic!* are the coolest. Ever. Thank you to all the supporters and readers, and an extra-special thank-you to these super *Blogtastic!* fans who put a smile on my face:

Asia Kalvelage, Jasmine A. Anderson, Anastasia Ervin, Alissa French, Halli Boman, Eric and Maddie Moss, Emily McLaughlin, Emmi Pargament, Hailey Cooper, Seraya Hamilton, Makayla DeMario, and Emily, Bethanie, and Annelise Borst.

WARNING!!!

This is not just any notebook. This is my super-secret Pre-Blogging Notebook! This is where I'll write all the super-juicy ~~gossip~~ ~~rumors~~ stuff I hear this summer so I can post about it later on my anonymous Blogtastic blog! After all, I wouldn't want to forget any important details, or accidentally post wrong information.

Who knows how many problems that might cause?

And right now it's one of THE most über-important times of the year—summer vacation! And even though I have no idea what I'll be doing this summer, I DO know that I'll be posting my best blog posts yet. My BFF, Nona Bows, says I'm too nosy sometimes, but really, I'm only conducting necessary research.

Also, we're going to be awesome seventh graders this year, so it's doubly important to make sure my blog hits popular status. That way, I can blog about me and Nona and other unpopulars so we can move up (way, way up!) on the popularity meter.

Now, if you're reading this and your name isn't Nona Bows (still, Nona, you said you wouldn't PURPOSELY read this either), then you are definitely snooping. Nobody likes a snooper. And I will have the fingerprints on this page traced (no lie, I bought a kit) so I will know exactly who you are.

Anything you buy online is guaranteed to work!

So you should just totally avoid this avoidable problem and stop reading immediately. That's right, just put this cleverly disguised ordinary-looking notebook down and forget you ever read this page. Forget that I'm going to find all the juiciest info this summer to blog about. Oh, and forget you know that I, Sofia Becker, am THE Blogtastic Blogger.

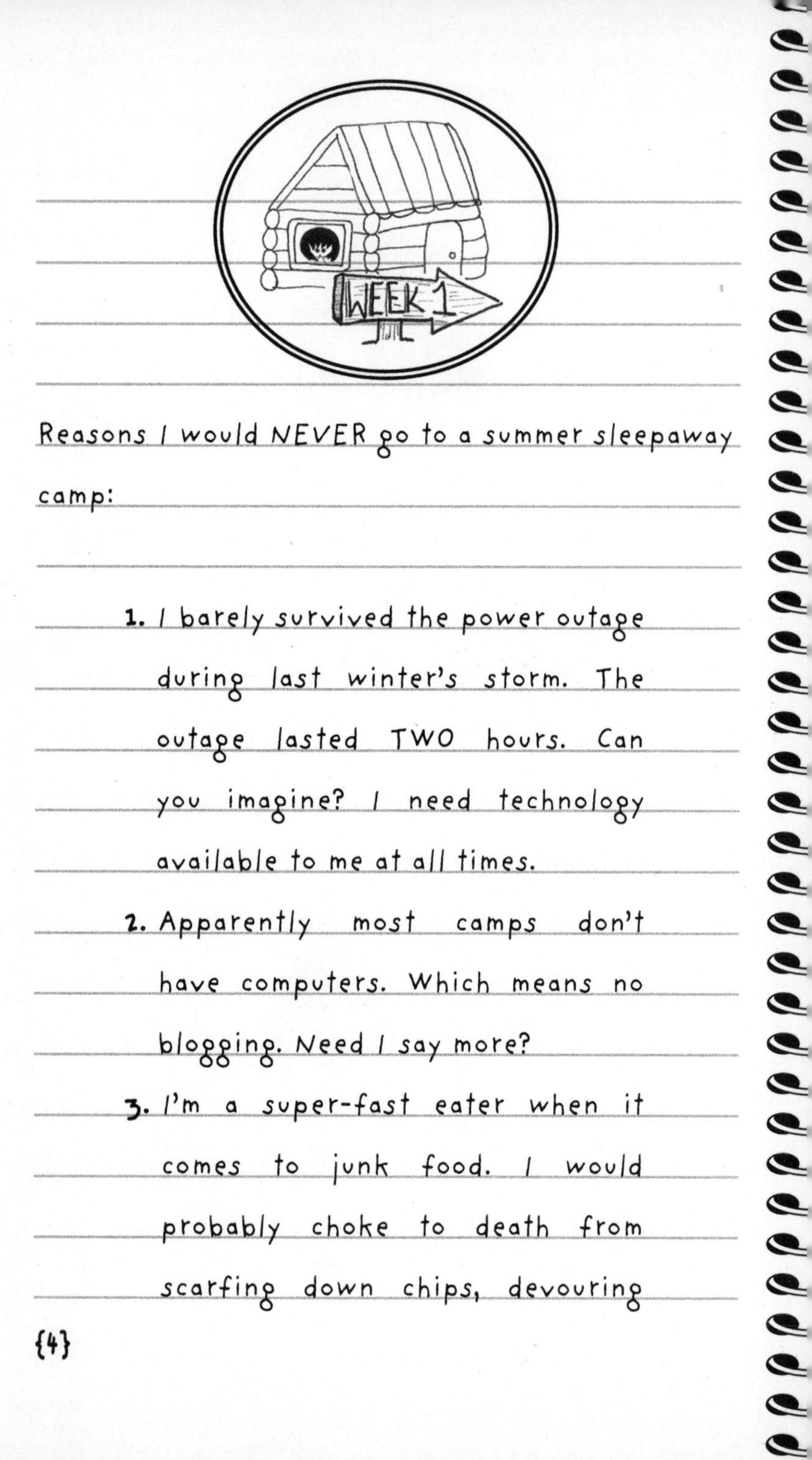

Reasons I would NEVER go to a summer sleepaway camp:

1. I barely survived the power outage during last winter's storm. The outage lasted TWO hours. Can you imagine? I need technology available to me at all times.
2. Apparently most camps don't have computers. Which means no blogging. Need I say more?
3. I'm a super-fast eater when it comes to junk food. I would probably choke to death from scarfing down chips, devouring

marshmallows, or inhaling hot dogs around the campfire.

4. The closest I've ever come to "roughing it" was watching that TV show *Survivor*.

And that one time I accidentally locked myself outside.
At night.
For an entire hour!

5. Creepy-crawlies! Bugs and I do NOT mix well.

HELP!

6. Being away from friends, family, and Sam Sam—the best parrot in the world—would be super-hard.

But despite these very valid reasons, here I am, sitting in the backseat of my dad's car with Nona for a three-hour-long ride to Krakatow, a four-week sleepaway camp. FOUR weeks! Yes, I was totally suckered into it.

It kind of happened this way:

My parents ~~asked~~ forced me to go. With my dad working so much and Mom taking care of Halli, my new baby sister, they didn't want me sitting around the house all summer bored out of my mind. They already think I spend too much time on the computer.

But the biggest deal was having Nona go too. She's totally not the camping type. I had to ask her about a million times to join me.

Me: Pleeeease go with me?

Nona: Um . . .

Me: Please?

Nona: Well, uh . . .

Me: C'mon! We'll have so much fun together!

Please?
Please? Please?
Please?
C'mon! You know I refuse to beg.
Please?

Nona: Will there be boys?

Me: The cutest boys. Ever.

Nona: Count me in!

Going to camp with Nona totally reeks of awesomeness.

Speaking of reeking . . . Nona thinks it's cute to air her feet in the car. With the windows rolled up. There should be a law against stink being confined in enclosed spaces.

Okay, so Mom can be totally embarrassing (especially considering that she's a teacher at my school), but sometimes it can't even compare to the ÜBER-embarrassment that oozes from my dad. Nona and I were locked in a car with him with the radio blasting, which was bad enough. The embarrassment began in the form of a music-induced seizure.

It started with the drumming of his fingers

on the steering wheel, which led to arm waving and neck swaying and ended with a serious head-nodding convulsion.

And then came . . . THE HUMMING!

He was so out of tune and totally clashed with the music so badly that it sounded as if the car was having engine problems.

Then came the worst part (yes, it gets worse) . . . THE SINGING!

I wish Dad were on the radio.
Then I could turn him OFF!

If anyone other than Nona had been in the car with us, I would have contemplated jumping out of the moving vehicle.

You know, if I could fly or something . . .

But Nona, who is used to my family craziness, and even expects it, just raised an eyebrow and said, "Lovely."

Which is code for "horrifically embarrassing beyond actual words."

1. "Interesting." Really means "Wow,

that is so dull I almost died of boredom."

2. "Genius." Really means "Horribly dumb beyond words (except when I say it)."
3. "I know what you mean." Really means "I haven't the slightest idea what you're talking about."
4. "What's that smell?" Really means "Why do you stink like that?"
5. "I'm tired." Really means "You're boring."
6. "Are you serious?" Really means "You can't possibly be serious."

I suppose there are worse things, though. I mean, Halli could be here wailing for the whole three hours (she cries A LOT). Luckily, she is in her ~~cage~~ crib at home with Mom.

I suppose falling off a cliff would be worse than listening to Dad's singing too.

Nona read her latest comic book while I played with my shoelaces.

How many ways can you say "boring"?

Although summer is an important time of year to keep your blog current, I will have to wait until after summer camp to make any updates. Which means my super-secret notebook is THAT much more important.

#1 reason why I'm happy to be going away to camp

Not to mention any names or anything, but . . .

No Mia St. Claire!

Even though she's away for the summer too. Apparently she's super-busy having a super-fun time at some super-fancy beach house.

She is THE most impossibly frustrating, most popular girl ever, with the shiniest locks of fruit-scented hair. She made sure nobody at school missed her news about her beach vacation.

"I'm going to slather on sunscreen and sunbathe because that's what you do when you're in a tropical location. And then I'll wash my hair with mango-pineapple-kiwi shampoo a bazillion times to get the sand out because that's what happens when you lie on the beach all day. And then I'll have sun-kissed locks that blow in the wind off my catamaran because that's what you do when you have an incredibly awesome vacation planned."

But I'm just thrilled to get away from her for the summer. And also from evil Penelope, who tries to make my life miserable.

Oh, and Mia's sidekick and best friend, Maddie, who has hair long enough to use as a weapon. Annoying much?

But that also means no Andrew this summer. He's only my biggest forever crush in the history of foreverness. Seriously, how will I ever survive the summer without seeing him?

No, I did NOT secretly take these photos while Nona was distracting him.

I think sleepaway camp will be the perfect opportunity to find the perfect blogging material and make my blog a ray of summer sunshine for all my readers.

FINALLY! WE ARRIVE AT CAMP!

THE CABINS

Holy zombie cows from Mars!

Apparently we are responsible for carrying all our camp gear on a one-mile hike just to get to the cabins.

A MILE!

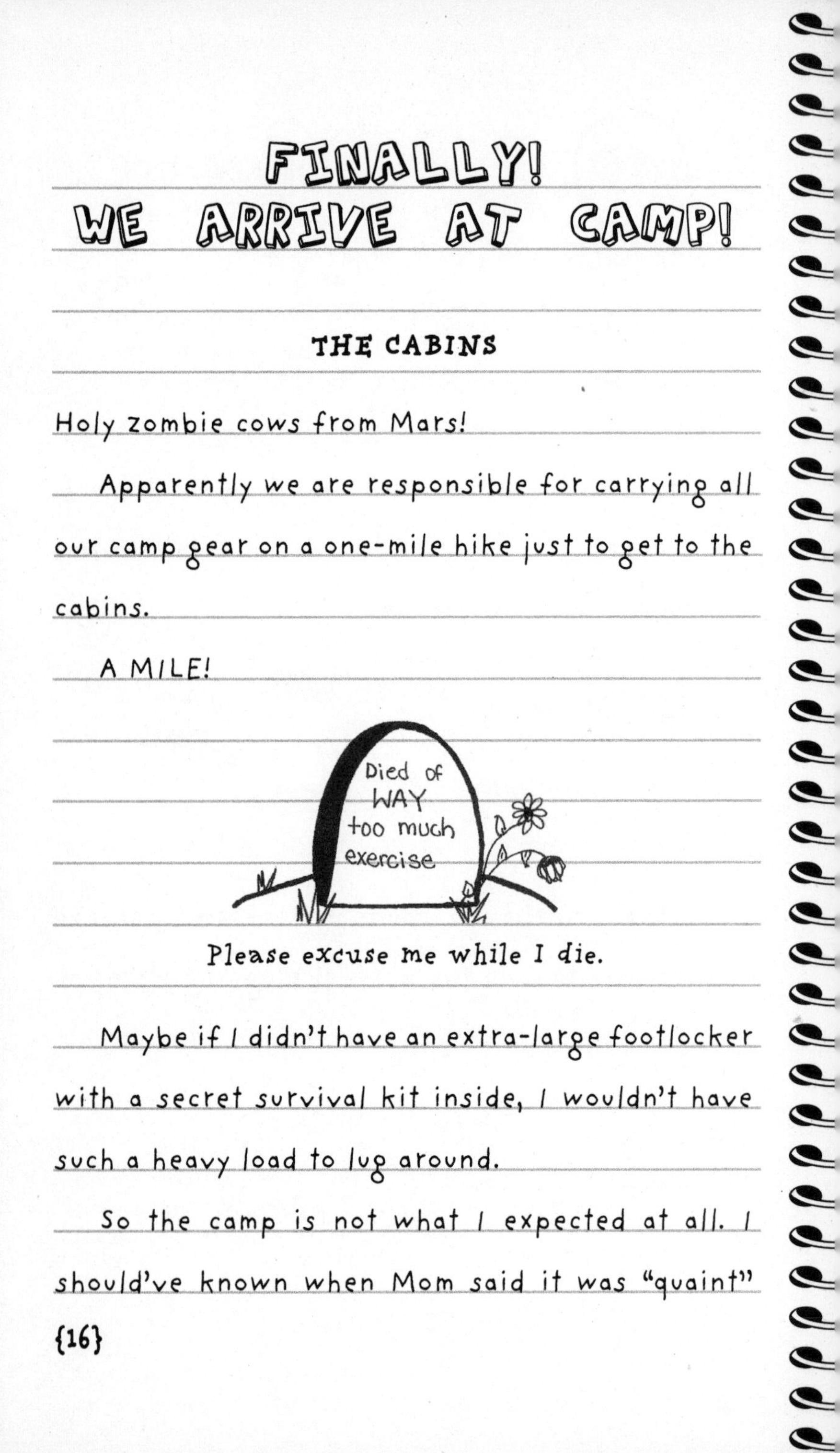

Please excuse me while I die.

Maybe if I didn't have an extra-large footlocker with a secret survival kit inside, I wouldn't have such a heavy load to lug around.

So the camp is not what I expected at all. I should've known when Mom said it was "quaint" and "full of character" that what she really meant was "tiny" and "old-fashioned."

And it's busy. Way busier than the shopping mall on a weekend. During the holidays.

Everywhere I look there are tons of kids hanging out. You would think Nona and I would be lost in the sea of people, but nope. Like a heat-seeking missile, a girl with glasses flew straight at us as soon as we reached the cabins. She was clasping a clipboard, wearing a whistle around her neck, and looking very "official."

"Official" is a nice way of saying "uptight."

She stopped abruptly in front of us and began pointing to her clipboard all crazy-like.

"You girls are late. Late! Punctuality is very important. The other campers have already started orientation!"

She was acting like the whole earth would shatter because we were ten minutes late. Normally I would say something like:

But apparently she's our counselor and she has

the authority to make our summer miserable. Her name tag says "Priscilla Jane" and I make the mistake of calling her just Priscilla.

Before she rushed off, she instructed us to put our luggage down and join everyone else for orientation.

Orientation is code for "Rules for NOT Having Fun."

A male counselor is going over the rules now.

Some of the rules are okay, and to be expected. Like . . .

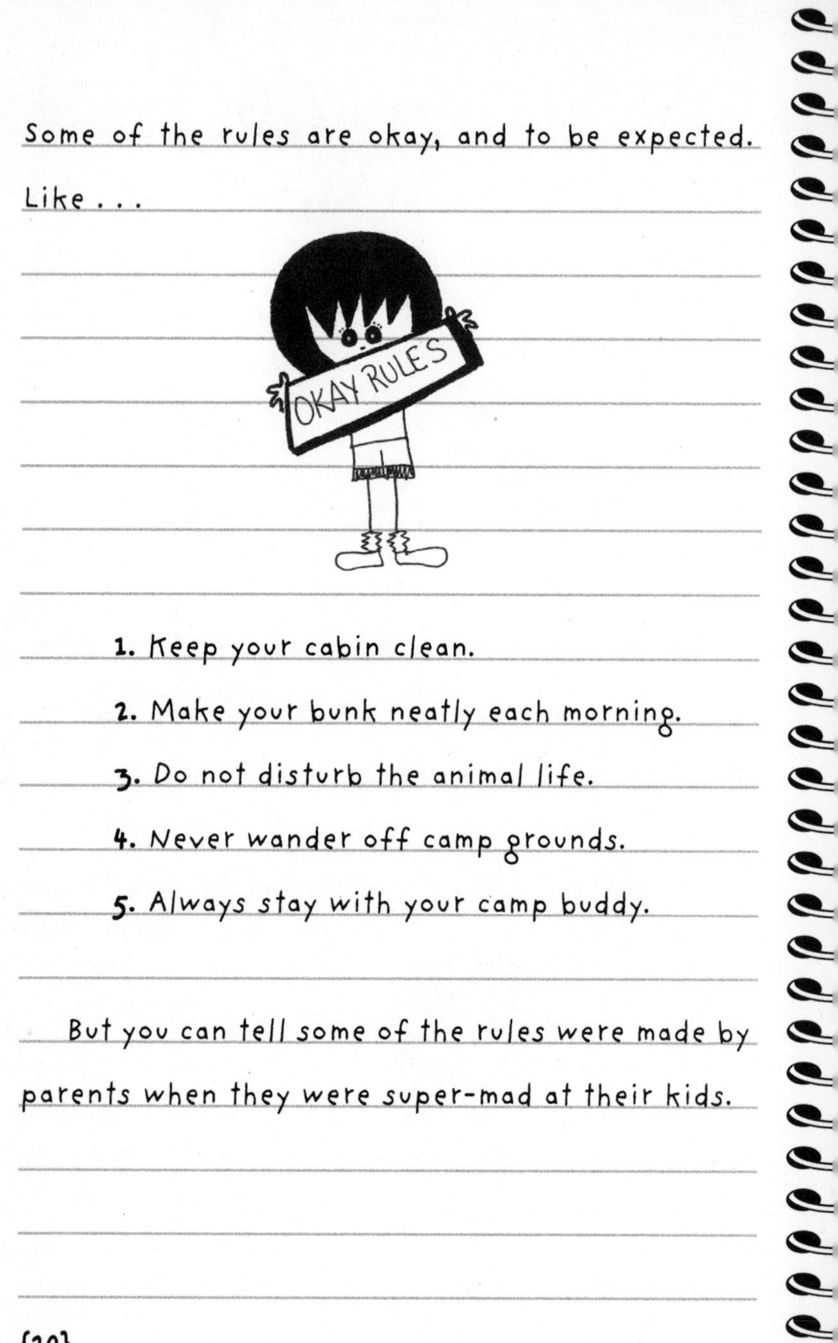

1. Keep your cabin clean.
2. Make your bunk neatly each morning.
3. Do not disturb the animal life.
4. Never wander off camp grounds.
5. Always stay with your camp buddy.

But you can tell some of the rules were made by parents when they were super-mad at their kids.

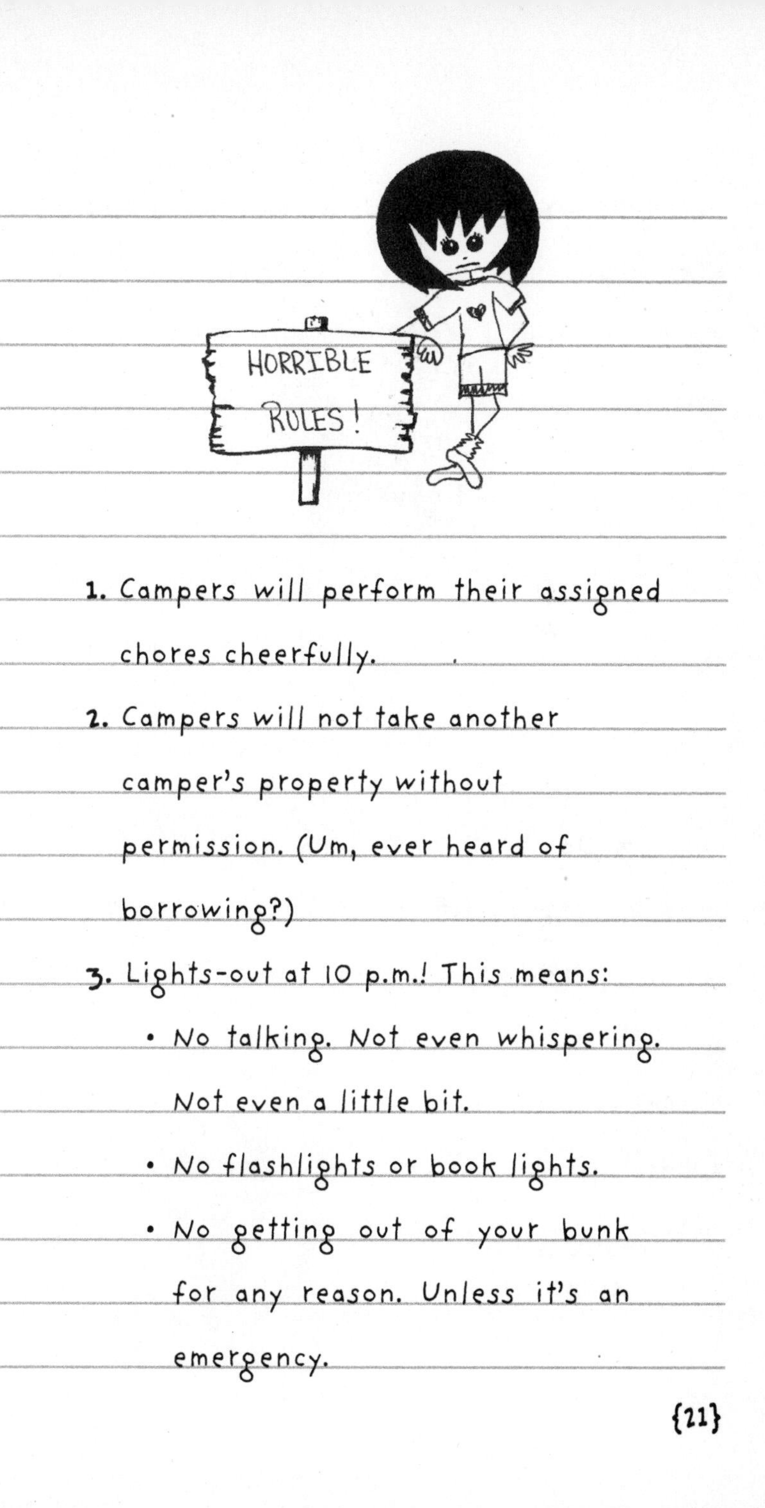

1. Campers will perform their assigned chores cheerfully.
2. Campers will not take another camper's property without permission. (Um, ever heard of borrowing?)
3. Lights-out at 10 p.m.! This means:
   - No talking. Not even whispering. Not even a little bit.
   - No flashlights or book lights.
   - No getting out of your bunk for any reason. Unless it's an emergency.

I look around and notice that most of the kids are whispering to their friends and not paying much attention. Except for Nona. She's taking this way serious.

She's even taking notes!

But I keep fidgeting and trying to guess which girls might be in my cabin. See, that's the good thing about going somewhere where nobody knows you.

You're a total stranger.

No one will know if you're popular. It's like summer camp erases all your middle-school history for those four weeks. Which means you can be anyone you want. Yes! You can reinvent yourself! So I'm going to totally popularize myself this summer.

COOLNESS CAMP EXPERIMENT

I will be Fancy Sofia Becker. Fancy like Mia St. Claire, and I will instantly have tons of friends. And everyone will love me. This should not be confused with admiration for Mia.

My secret survival kit—which is actually a messenger bag my aunt gave me for my birthday—includes everything I need to fully take on this extremely challenging role. Some of the stuff I have:

1. Lots of hair accessories. I've been studying fashion magazines for, like, a whole five days already,

and I came up with some cute new hairstyles.

2. Froufrou fruity sprays. My parents got me a scent called Outrageous Orange, but because I wanted something even more tropical-smelling, I came up with the brilliant idea to make a spray of my own. I call it Perky Pineapple. The secret ingredient? Actual pineapple juice! Who knows, I could even come out with my own line of sprays!

3. Super-shiny lip gloss. Okay, so I did buy some Lip Smackers, but I really wanted to punch up the shine. Nona read in one of my magazines that Vaseline makes lips super-shiny. She came up with the idea to actually put a thin layer of Vaseline over the Lip

Smackers, so I took a jar from my baby sister's room.

4. Magazines. Yes, I will continue my research during free time at camp so I can carry some of this newfound fashion creativity into the seventh grade.
5. A big bow. I really had to convince myself to bring this. I'm SO not a bow type of girl. But I decided if I was gonna wear one, I might as well make it the most super-awesomest-looking bow. Ever.

Nona ALWAYS wears a flower in her hair, so she

said she'll just wear a different type of flower. I told her that's not being someone different.

"Yes, it is," she said. "Because it will be a type of flower I'd normally never wear."

Then she asked me to make her one that matches my bow.

We'll practically be twins!

While Counselor Guy drones on about how Camp Krakatow (which strangely sounds exactly like Crack-A-Toe) is named after a lake and fills us in on the history of the land and blah blah blah, my ears perk up when I hear about "The Beast."

Yes, all the camp buildings (except the cabins) are named after an imaginary hairy monster.

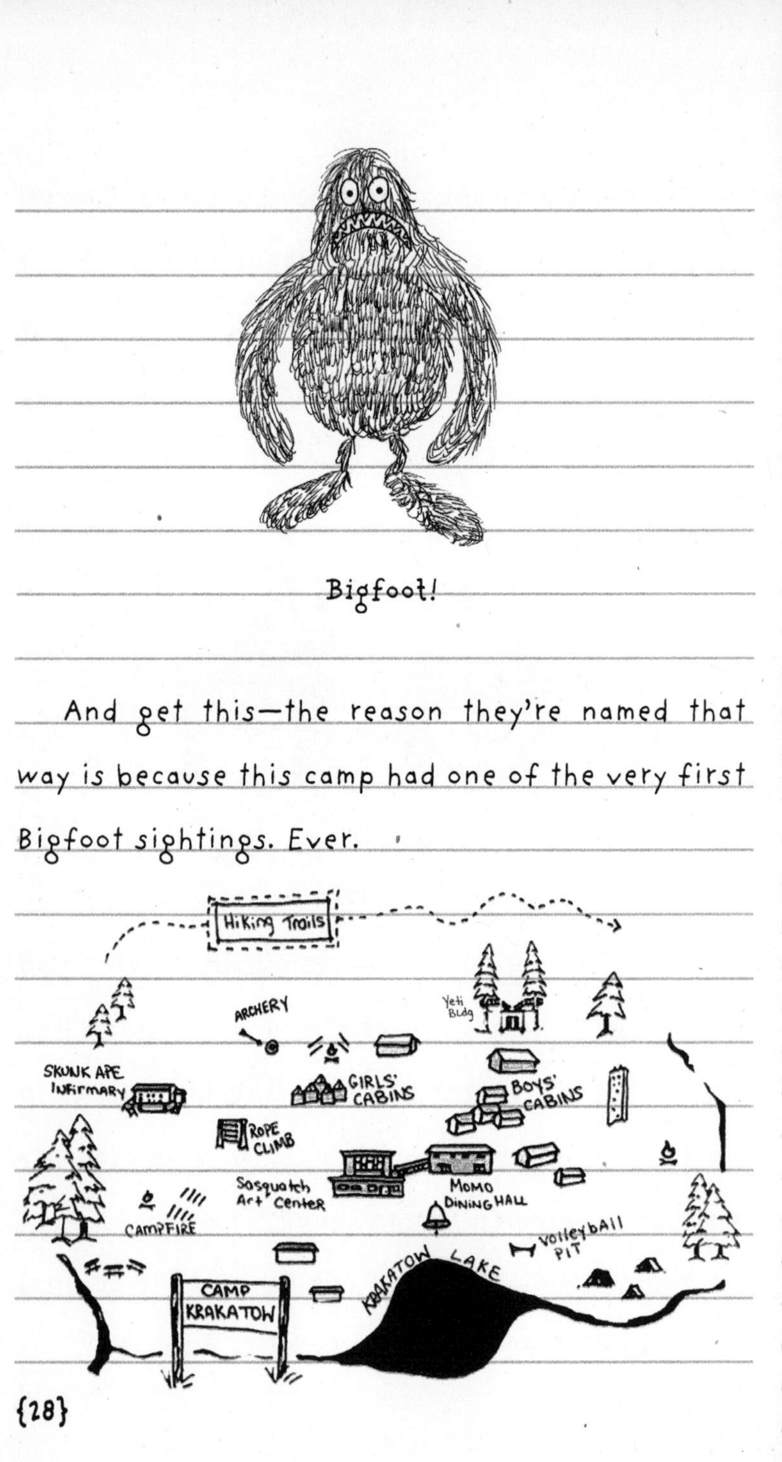

Bigfoot!

And get this—the reason they're named that way is because this camp had one of the very first Bigfoot sightings. Ever.

Counselor Guy goes back into boring talk, about how it's just a legend and blah blah blah. But I know better. And I have an idea.

A brilliant idea to discover Bigfoot!

CABIN ASSIGNMENTS!

Five counselors and the counselors in training (CITs) line up in front of us.

"Okay," says Priscilla Jane, aka The Priss, as she taps her pen on the edge of her clipboard. "Each cabin is named after a butterfly. You will be given your butterfly name and then group up accordingly. Understand?"

A couple of nods, but no one really answers.

"I can't hear you!" yells The Priss.

Is it just my imagination, or is she staring right at me as she yells that?

"Yes!" everyone yells back. Including me. But only because I was feeling threatened.

One by one the other counselors (who seem way nicer than The Priss) call out the names of the cabins: Monarchs. Queens. Peacocks. And Painted Ladies. "Sofia," says The Priss. "You are in . . ."

Are you kidding me? My cabin is named after something an old person has.

Or what my mom complains about after I stress her out too much . . .

But suddenly my attention turns to Nona as her name is called and she walks to the group standing NEXT to me. Not WITH me.

What? We aren't even in the same cabin?

This sudden news is causing me to become cranky.

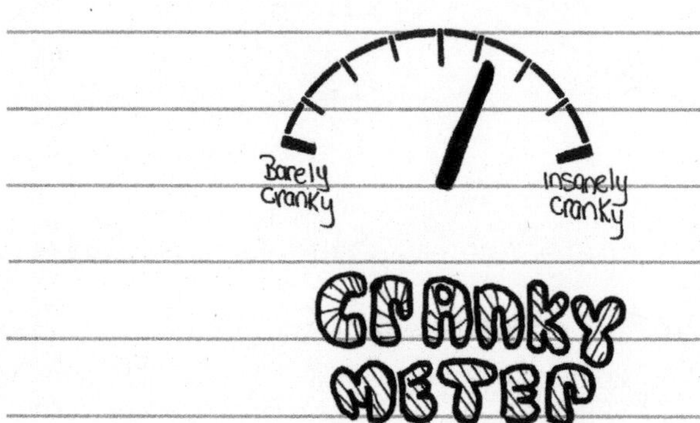

Nona looks happy as she walks to her group, though. And I can't blame her. She's got plenty of reasons to be happy. For instance, she has a nice counselor, while I have The Priss.

And also? She's a Queen.

I hope she doesn't let this go to her head.

COOLNESS EXPERIMENT

This experiment is really not cool at all. In fact, I'm practically sweating to death. The bow I made is super-hot. Especially when outside, in the scorching summer sun. Some of the girls in my cabin look at me like sweating is some sort of illness or something.

See? Isn't it totally normal for bows to wilt and sweat too?

And then I realize that they're really staring at me because my sweat caused the dye from the bow to somehow get on my skin.

That's NOT the type of attention I was hoping for.

I don't know why the dye would come off like that. Maybe it has something to do with the bow being in the dollar bin at the store?

Mia St. Claire would never be caught sweating.

But knowing Mia, her bows are probably made with some super-lightweight material that costs an outrageous amount of money and probably isn't as suffocating as mine.

So I decide I can do without the bow and still be fancy-ish.

MEANWHILE . . .

All of Nona's cabinmates are oohing and aahing over her perfectly made flower. I refuse to become jealous.

This is NOT my jealous face. It's my. . . I refuse to be jealous face. Yeah, that's it.

At least for today

THE GRAY HAIRSTREAKS CABIN

As I go through my things and finish unpacking, I notice a lot of the other girls' trunks are painted bright colors. Some have really cool designs, and others have lots of awesome decals. Mine looks so boring and plain compared to theirs. Maybe

I'll have a chance to do something about that while I'm here.

I pull out my pink fluffy pillow and my cupcake pillow and throw them both on my bunk.

"Ooh!" says a girl behind me. I turn around as she starts bouncing up and down, clapping.

I'm not sure what to say, since she keeps talking and talking and doesn't seem to take a breath.

"Oh, I'm Gabrielle. But you can call me Gabby for short. I'm a second-year. You must be a first-year because I don't remember you. And I would definitely remember someone with an ultracool cupcake pillow!"

Gabby's squealing gets the attention of the other girls in the cabin and they crowd around to see what the commotion is about.

"I have a red retro pillow that I take everywhere with me," says a girl named Makayla as she holds it up.

"Mine," says Bethanie, "is a patchwork pillow. My grandma made it for me."

Suddenly, it's like show-and-tell for pillows. Everyone is comparing their pillows and passing them around to the other girls.

Until in clomps a red-haired girl with a headful of bobbing curls that remind me of little springs. The room gets totally quiet as she claims the bunk above mine, tossing her stuff onto it angrily. She never once looks at any of us. It kind of kills our fun. Everyone goes back to their bunks and finishes unpacking. I swear Rude Girl says "stupid pillows" under her breath too.

Great. Out of everyone, she has to be my bunk buddy. At least I got the bottom bunk, next to a window that faces the boys' cabins.

THAT JUST HAPPENED QUITE BY ACCIDENT. . . .

RANDOM CAMP OBSERVATION

Summer is definitely a time to meet new people. One thing I've learned about new people? Anyone who stomps around in big ol' boots in the middle of summer definitely has issues. Like, the angry and rude kind. And also, butterflies are ugly. All of them. Just sayin'.

CABIN CONTEST

Our first group activity is to work together with our cabinmates in a contest. We have to make creative signs for our cabins, using our butterfly names, which will be displayed above each cabin door. Winners get to leave five minutes early for dinner.

The boys are having the same contest on their

side of camp. I think the counselors tell us this so we'll really participate and try to win.

Bethanie and Gabby have a ton of ideas and it's hard to pick just one. I mean, how can you make a sign look good with the words "Gray" and "Hairstreaks" on it? So we do the opposite and draw a bunch of colorful, bright butterflies.

Rude Girl shot down all our other ideas.

The other cabins do a pretty good job too. The Peacocks make butterflies around their name, but the wings look like actual peacock feathers.

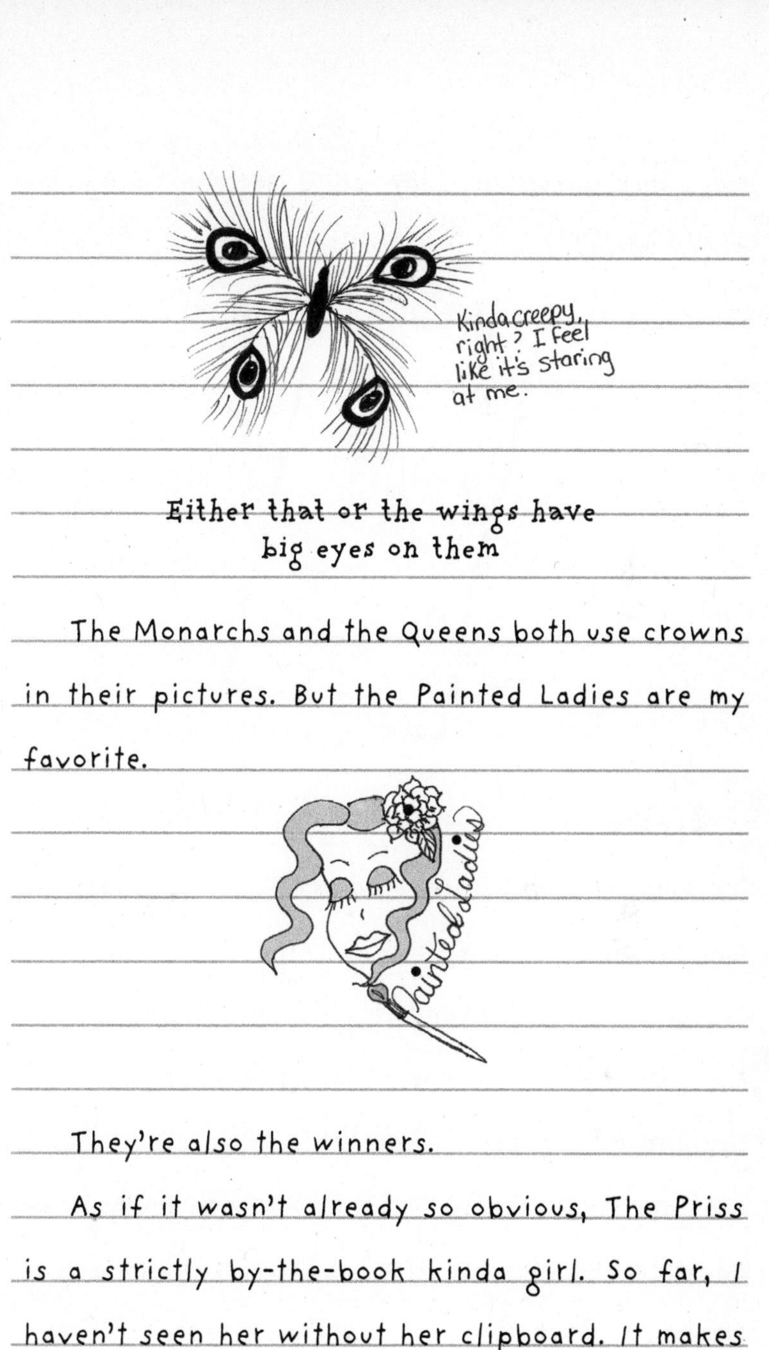

Either that or the wings have big eyes on them

The Monarchs and the Queens both use crowns in their pictures. But the Painted Ladies are my favorite.

They're also the winners.

As if it wasn't already so obvious, The Priss is a strictly by-the-book kinda girl. So far, I haven't seen her without her clipboard. It makes me a bit paranoid. Like she's writing down my every move.

Sofia was suddenly walking to the cabins.

Sofia talking to Nona. Very suspicious.

Sofia blinked four times in the last 30 seconds.

Before going to the dining hall, The Priss ~~tells~~ lectures us about how important it is to keep our cabins clean and follow all the rules, because every cabin is rewarded with merit points for their behavior. The cabin with the most merits at the end of the four weeks gets to go on a super-fun (and super-secret) field trip with one of the boys' cabins. How did I miss hearing that part at orientation?

Our CIT, Khloe, who is like a mini-me of our counselor, is just as annoying as The Priss. She even has a mini clipboard.

"Line up, girls! Straight lines. C'mon."

Rude Girl rolls her eyes, pretty much like she does to everyone else, and grabs her notebook before going to the very back of the line.

Her name is actually Olivia. But the weird thing? Her notebook says "Madison" on it. Why is she carrying around a notebook with another girl's name on it? She takes it EVERYWHERE.

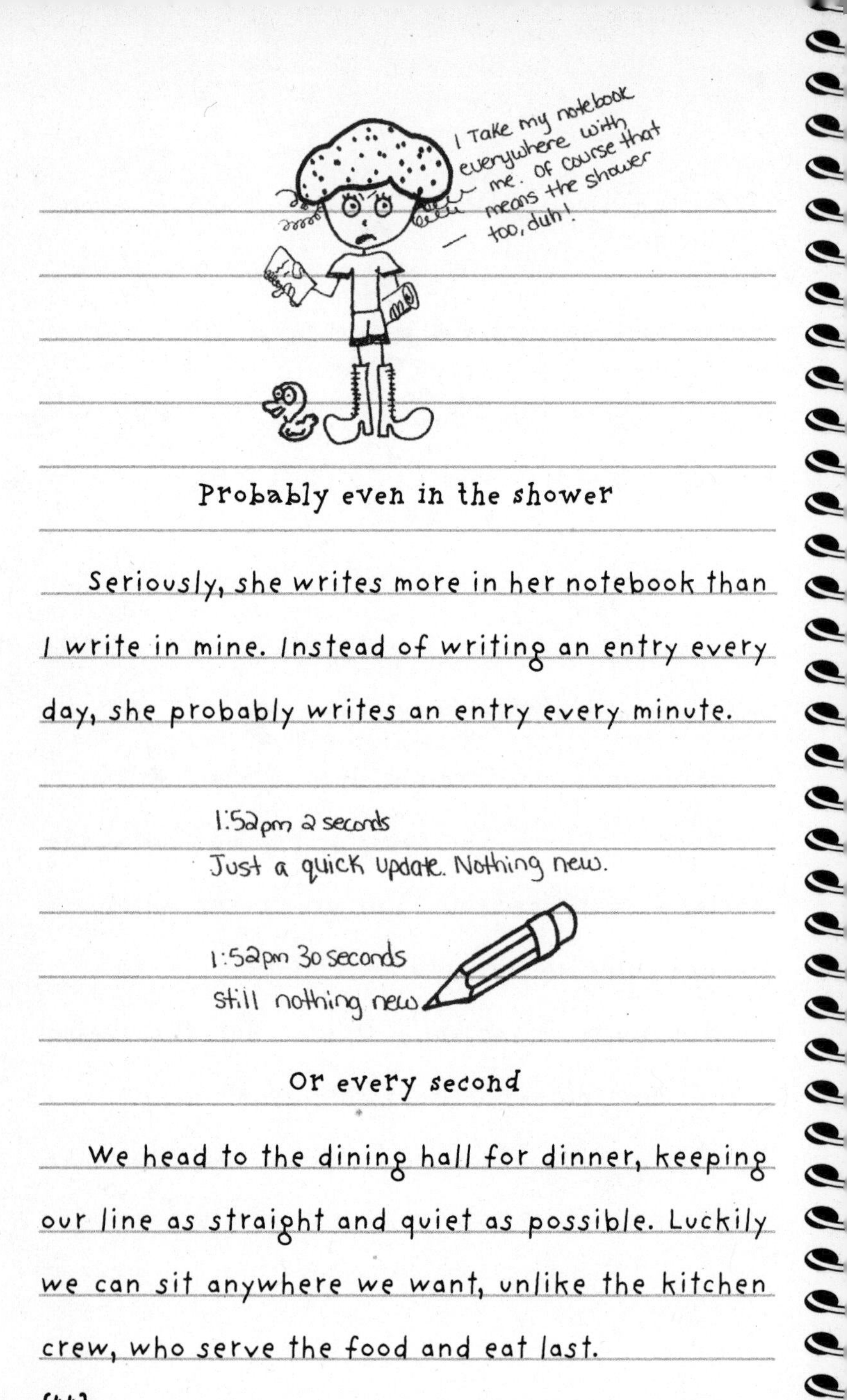

Probably even in the shower

Seriously, she writes more in her notebook than I write in mine. Instead of writing an entry every day, she probably writes an entry every minute.

1:52pm 2 seconds
Just a quick update. Nothing new.

1:52pm 30 seconds
Still nothing new.

Or every second

We head to the dining hall for dinner, keeping our line as straight and quiet as possible. Luckily we can sit anywhere we want, unlike the kitchen crew, who serve the food and eat last.

The dining hall looks pretty much like our school cafeteria, except it's a cabin. And the food tastes pretty much like cafeteria food, except not as bland. And it's healthier.

Doesn't anyone realize you can make healthy food taste way better?

Most of the boys are sitting on one side of the room, while the girls are on the other. I look over at Nona to see if she notices.

Nona's inhaling her food like she hasn't eaten in a month.

Olivia is sitting at the end of our table not even touching her tray. Instead, she's writing in her notebook.

I walk over to her and ask, all politely, what she's writing that is just so super-incredibly important. She gives me a mean look and tells me to mind my own business.

WORST. MORNING. EVER.

What's worse than waking up early for school? How about waking up super-early for camp? And instead of being woken up by a beeping alarm, how about waking up to a giant clanging bell tethered to a tree that not only scares you out of your sleep but also gives you a headache?

As soon as I remember where I am, I grab my shower bag and head to the bathroom.

The Gray Hairstreaks have to share a bathroom with the Monarchs. To get to it, you actually have to go outside. It's not really a big deal, since it's just on the other side of our cabin. But it seems more like a mile away since it's freezing out.

Each shower stall has a super-thin curtain. They're really more like small dressing rooms at a clothing store.

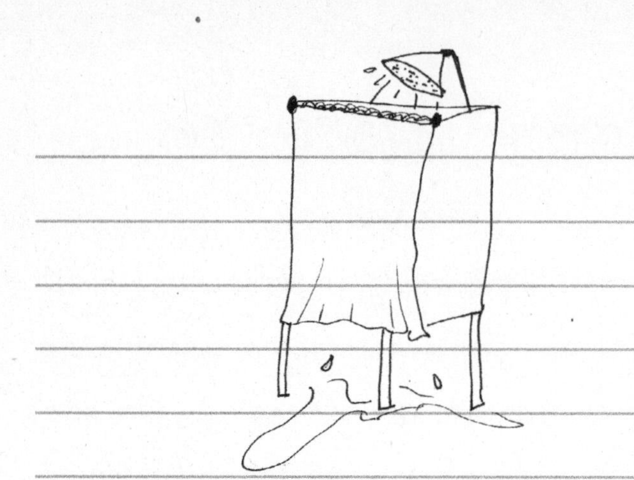

The wind blows into the bathroom as I push open the door. It's very hard to see. It's kind of scary.

More girls file in after I get into the shower, and within five minutes it seems as if everyone from both cabins is there, complaining about having to wait.

But the absolute worst is that I end up having to take a shower with this creepy-looking beetle on the stone wall next to me. I hold my breath, careful not to move too much. But it's hard because the water goes from lukewarm to cold in about five seconds flat.

After I get out, some girl pushes past me to claim the stall. "You better have saved some hot water," she growls.

Ha. She's in for a treat.

We've been assigned shower cubbies to put our things in (well, whatever fits, anyway). I can barely squeeze my hair dryer in there. After I towel off and get dressed and somewhat warm, CIT Khloe announces our group activity back in the cabin.

"Today is the swim test," she says all snooty-like. "You and the Tiger Beetles will be taking it at the same time."

"Tiger Beetles?" asks Makayla.

Khloe sighs and says, "You know, the boys' cabin. You're named after butterflies, they're beetles."

She glares at us like we should've known this already, which makes me decide not to ask her why we had to shower if she knew we were going straight into the lake.

After we put our swimsuits on, we are instructed to grab our towels and go. The Priss takes over and yells at us about the importance of punctuality.

"C'mon, ladies, let's get moving!" Then she blows her whistle, which I swear she points directly at my ear. On purpose.

We walk down the sloping hill to the lake. The boys are already in the water, and there are four counselors. Basically, if we can keep afloat and pass a few simple tests, then we're approved for all water activities without having to take swimming lessons.

And I don't mean to brag, but I have pretty mean swimming skills. Nona and I took lessons when we were, like, three, and even then I was moved to an advanced class early on. I wouldn't be surprised if I was part fish.

Actually, it would depend on
which part of the fish. . . .

Maybe "fish" isn't the right word to use. I bet Mia would say something fancier. Like "beautiful mermaid princess."

or "delicate dolphin."

We stand in the shallow end, dunking our heads underwater and floating on our backs. We take turns swimming to a buoy and back, which really doesn't seem far at all. Then, to finish up, all we need to do is tread water for two minutes.

I look at the girl next to me, who happens to be Olivia. I shrug. "I can tread for five minutes with one leg tied behind my back," I say. She kind of smirks at me, but that's okay. People usually react that way when they're jealous.

"Ready?" yells one of the counselors. "Start!"

The moment I kick my leg out, a sharp, stabbing pain shoots through it.

I scream and grab my calf. Did something bite me? I stick my head underwater but I can't see

anything. Actually, I don't even have the chance to see anything, because before I fully realize what's happening, I'm swooped up from the water. The shock causes me to inhale water up my nose.

"Code yellow!" I hear someone shout.

"What's a code yellow?" I say to the counselor who's pulling me to the edge of the lake.

I'm coughing and choking. I am also completely stunned at what just happened.

"Emergency," she tells me. "You almost drowned."

"No, I didn't! I'm fine," I tell her.

She says I need to sit out the rest of the time to rest.

I don't see what the big deal is. I got a leg cramp.

Or maybe I was almost attacked by a vicious sea creature.

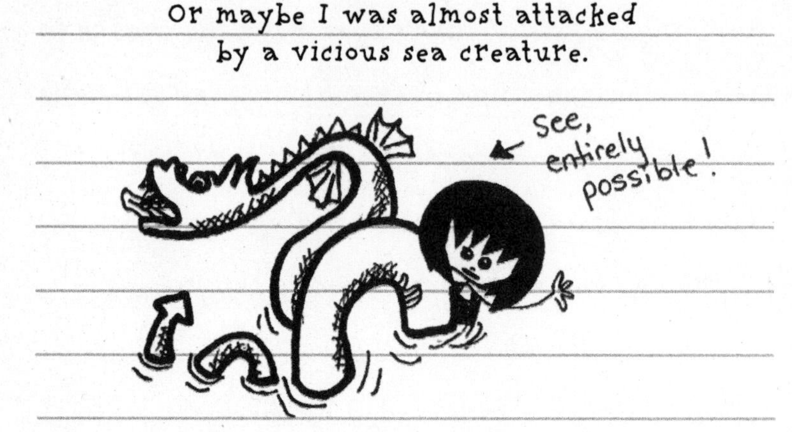

But I definitely wasn't drowning. I could've even touched the bottom if I wanted!

My leg is still sore, so I limp up to the rock where I left my beach towel and snatch it up, shaking it out and wrapping it around myself.

As I squeeze the water from my hair, I hear a low rumble of laughter. I glance up and notice that everyone is looking straight at me.

What's wrong with me? Why are they all laughing?

Oh, no! My mom packed the towels I used back when I was in swim class with Nona. I can't believe this. I had some super-cute new ones for camp.

"Turn it inside out," Olivia says under her breath.

Was Olivia really pulling an act of niceness at that moment?

The counselors blow their whistles to get everyone's attention, even though I still notice a few stares. I just hope nobody remembers any of this.

ARTS AND CRAFTS

At least Nona and I get to share some activities. As soon as she sees me she says:

"And I almost drowned," I say.

"But you really had on a SpongeBob towel?" she asks.

I frown. "Does that really matter? I was almost eaten by a sea creature! But it worked out because I was able to retest and pass."

We're outside the Sasquatch Art Center, where we are instructed to use anything found in nature to make something creative. Good thing my middle name is Creativity.

Nona starts digging through a pile of leaves. I have no idea what she's searching for.

"How do you like the girls in your cabin?" I ask her, wanting to change the subject.

"They're great!" she says a little too enthusiastically. I give her my one-raised-eyebrow look.

"Really?"

"Yes, really. There are even twin girls, Izzy and Inna, who are super-cool. They say everything at the same time. It's like they share a brain or something."

I collect a pile of sticks, thinking maybe I can build something creative with them.

This could totally be a stick building!

"One of the girls in my cabin seems to hate me," I confess. "Actually, she seems to hate everybody."

I tell Nona all about Olivia.

She shrugs. "Maybe she just doesn't like being away from home."

"Maybe."

"My counselor is the best," Nona says. "She's way cool. She lets us stay up a little past curfew if we're really quiet."

I don't even know where to begin with telling her about The Priss. But I don't have to say anything: the word is already out.

"I heard your counselor is the worst!" Nona says. "Way too strict and uptight. Too bad you're not in my cabin."

By the time the whistle blows for us to go inside and start making our crafts, I notice Nona has collected a large stick, some feathers, and a few leaves, while I'm just holding a small tree branch.

But I don't give up. I could still make something totally awesome.

Inside the art center, there are tables with glue, glitter, string, pom-poms, stickers, and a bunch of other things to glamorize our projects.

I grab the bottle of glue between me and Bethanie and start slathering it all over my tree branch. I'm still not sure what I'm making.

I then grab some loose glitter and sprinkle it over the branch. As I do this, I notice some of the glitter sticking to my fingertips. I look for something to wipe my hands with, but the closest thing I can find is tissue paper. Neon orange tissue paper, to be exact. The moment I grab it, I know it's a mistake.

It sticks to my hands!

I try to pull it off, but it tears and leaves pieces still stuck to my fingertips.

Nona sees what I'm going through and laughs loud enough to draw the attention of the other kids around us. Including a few of the boys. I know my cheeks turn bright red, because I can feel the heat rising to my face.

I shove my hands in my pockets, hoping not to draw any more attention to myself.

The whistle blows and Nona's counselor, Jessica, quiets the room down to get our attention.

I look down at my somewhat glittery tree branch. Ugh. What a mess. What am I going to say?

When Jessica gets to our table, Nona picks up her craft, a long, skinny stick fully decorated with feathers, leaves, glitter, and ribbon. I have to admit, it's pretty cool. "It's a customized wand," she says, holding it up.

After lots of oohing and aahing, some girl yells out:

Then Nona and everyone else turn their attention to me. I hold up my branch and my voice comes out in a squeak.

"This is my . . . uh . . . ah . . ."

For once I can't think on the spot. My brain has gone numb and I just stand there staring stupidly at this branch-thing.

Bethanie leans over and whispers in my ear, then places something in my hand.

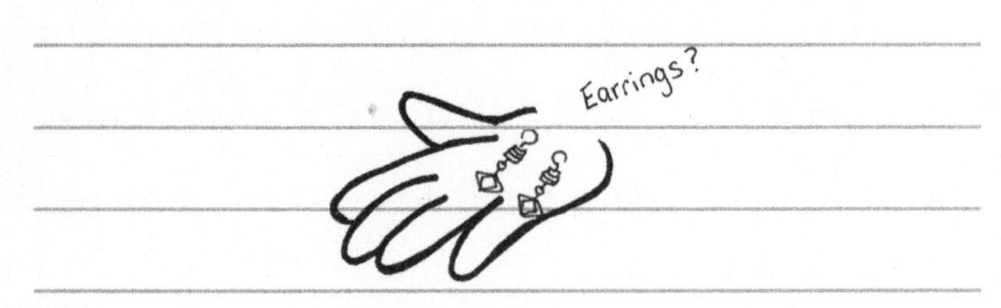

I flash her a huge smile and put the earrings on the branch, holding it up proudly.

"This is an earring tree!"

A few people say things like "How original" and "How creative." Just when I think everything has ended well, some boy shouts:

Hey! Look at her fingers!

Everyone starts laughing and I do the only thing I can do.

I laugh with them, hoping it will cover up how embarrassed I really am. Again.

* * *

So it really shouldn't come as a surprise that I would get injured my first week at a camp that sounds like Crack-A-Toe.

It was like one minute it wasn't there, and the next minute POOF! It suddenly appeared.

Olivia put down her notebook to help me up. I was almost speechless. This was the second time she was being nice to me!

"You really should watch where you're going," she said all snotty-like, which totally contradicted her helpful gesture.

I think I probably broke my ankle. Or my foot. All I know for sure is when I tried to put my weight on it, there was MAJOR PAIN. And I'm talking more than just the Mia St. Claire type of major pain.

I lop (limp-hop) my way to the nurse's cabin. The nurse tells me that I did not in fact break anything. It's just a sprain. Nothing an ice pack can't help. So I sit down on a cot with my leg elevated. And as the ice starts melting, it somehow springs a leak or something, because the next thing I know, two very embarrassing things happen, almost as suddenly as that tree stump appeared out of nowhere:

1. I'm sitting in a puddle of water.
2. A super-cute boy walks into the cabin, looking right at me.

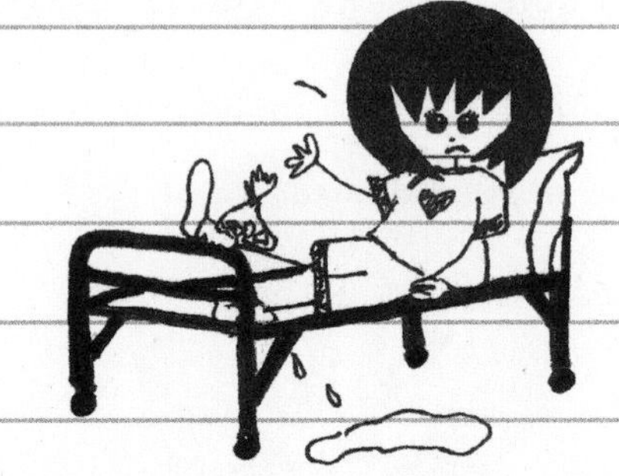

I try to act like sitting in a puddle is absolutely normal.

But what's even more embarrassing is that the cute boy notices my problem and grabs some paper towels.

I find out that the cute boy's name is Jackson and I might kinda overhear, while he's talking to the camp nurse, about his medical situation too. I say kinda because Jackson has a deep voice, so when he talks it's like a low murmur. I did hear him say "sumac," whatever that is.

The nurse thought I was being overdramatic about all the limping, but I assured her I was really in pain and I still wouldn't be surprised if my ankle was actually really broken. I thought I would get to lie in bed for a while, but nope. She gave me a set of crutches left behind by a camper from last summer. Crutches! Now everyone will know what a total klutz I am!

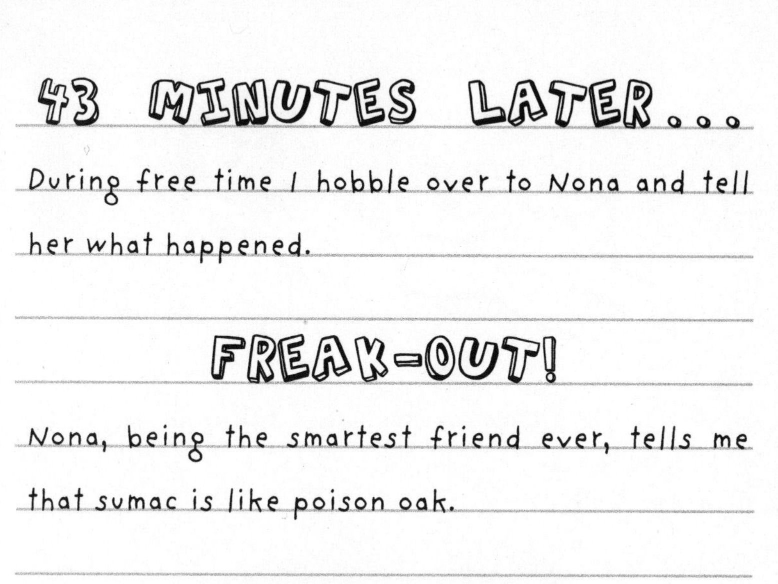

43 MINUTES LATER...

During free time I hobble over to Nona and tell her what happened.

FREAK-OUT!

Nona, being the smartest friend ever, tells me that sumac is like poison oak.

POISON OAK!

You know what that means, right?

I have poison oak!!!

Jackson handed me sumac-infested paper towels! And I touched them!

So my first instinct is to throw myself into the lake.

Or throw Jackson into the lake

But then Nona points out some random facts about this sumac stuff. Like since I didn't wash my hands right away, it's probably too late to do anything. If I have it, I have it.

I can already feel my skin becoming itchy.

CAMPFIRE FRIDAYS

Tonight we get to sit around a campfire and sing silly songs and tell ghost stories and probably even roast marshmallows.

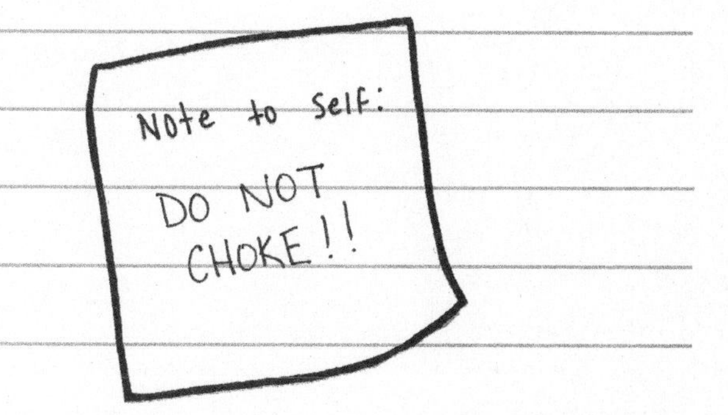

It's pretty cool having all the cabins at the campfire. It's the perfect time to scope everyone out.

One cute boy, who shall remain nameless, actually talked to me!

He basically said to me:

And I looked into his super-cute eyes and said:

And just like that, he gave me the bag of marshmallows to pass around.

But the point is, he asked ME.

And then I started to itch my skin like crazy, which caused him to look at me kind of weird. So I muttered something about how I have a mosquito bite. I hope he heard, because I really don't want anyone knowing that I probably have poison oak, because then everyone will make a point of staying away from me.

The counselors had us sing silly songs that

were more like dumb songs (there was one about a monkey and a tree) and then told a few ghost stories that spooked me a bit too much. Olivia told one about a witch who was a watcher in the woods at a summer camp.

The girls were more into it than the boys, though. The boys seemed to be having some sort of side competition on who could fit the most marshmallows into their mouths.

It was so funny, I pointed it out to Nona. But I kinda accidentally pointed toward a group of girls with a roasted marshmallow on the tip of my stick. And, well, you know . . . one thing led to another and my marshmallow kind of sort of flew off and smacked Olivia right in her springy red curls.

Was it my fault she was sitting
right in my line of view?

Boy, did she scream!

Rude Girl has a set of lungs!

Before I knew what was happening, marshmallows were flying in all directions. One even pegged me in my eye, and I was slinging them around too. The Priss got in the middle of it all to break it up and I, well . . . I kinda hit her with one of the marshmallows.

But that's what happens when you stand in the middle of a burnt-marshmallow fight, right?

We lost so many merit points, we might even be in the negative numbers now.

ANCIENT STUFF

Today we had to watch videos. On this thing called a VCR. I don't know what that's all about, but the videos were super-old. Possibly even older than my parents, because the picture quality totally sucked. It was all grainy and reminded me of one of those old photos your parents keep that turns yellowish with age.

But anyway, it was hard to pay attention to Nature Is Your Best Friend. Basically the video told us about every tree, bird, bug, and lake that has ever existed.

And that was followed by a second video. I don't remember the name, but it was something like How Not to Get Eaten by a Bear. Did you know that there are actual rules to follow if you're approached by a bear? And that they are showing this to us the day AFTER we camped outside with these killer bears? Our parents paid to send us to a camp with actual bears?!

With my luck, I'll run into a rabid bear who likes chocolate even more than I do.

I started to fall asleep until Nona nudged me with her sharp, bony elbow and passed me a note.

Nona is the sweetest! She totally remembers how much I love note writing. And it definitely helps to get my mind off my poison oak.

So I write back. And then she writes back. And after a while we kind of have this longish note with funny doodles about the other campers and

I decide to tuck it inside my notebook because it will make a totally good souvenir.

SOFIA!!! This is SOOOO boring!

zzz ← me

I know, right? Hey, can you hear that guy next to me? He's a LOUD breather!!

HaHa :) maybe the Blogtastic Blogger can post something about that when we get back home!

Nah, I need to write about something funnier than that. Like maybe if he snorted a bug up his nose while breathing or something

EWWW!!

Back →

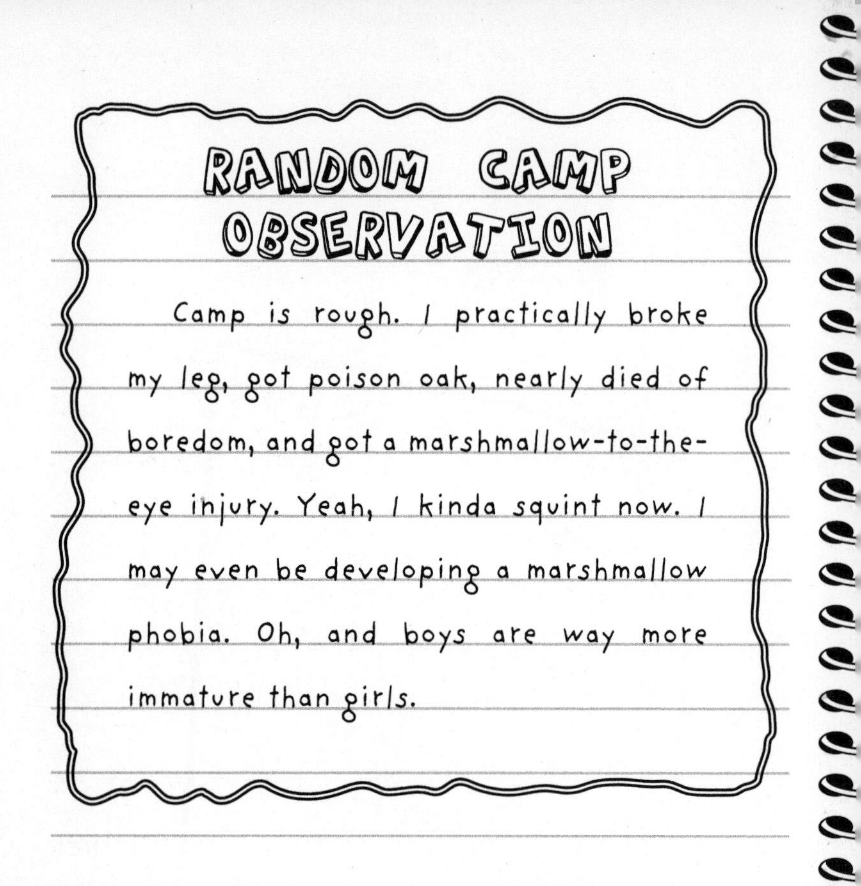

RANDOM CAMP OBSERVATION

Camp is rough. I practically broke my leg, got poison oak, nearly died of boredom, and got a marshmallow-to-the-eye injury. Yeah, I kinda squint now. I may even be developing a marshmallow phobia. Oh, and boys are way more immature than girls.

YOU'VE GOT MAIL!

Most of us got mail today. Care packages from home, to be exact. I so wasn't expecting this! I haven't even written one letter home yet. I will definitely have to do that right away.

Nona got a package from her mom too, so we sat down under the shade of a large tree by her cabin to open them.

Right away, we could tell our moms had prepared the packages together.

Dead giveaway: everything is the same!

Well, almost. Mine had a handwritten note from Mom and a picture of Halli making a funny face. Nona got a bag of candy! All our favorite kinds. Yes, I said "our," because her note said to share some with me.

Aside from that, we also got:

- Decals for our trunks (yay!)
- A Squeeze Breeze mister fan
- Glow-in-the-dark friendship bracelets
- Insect repellent to wear around our wrists (which I totally won't be using, by the way. I'll probably just use it in the shower).

☆ ☆ ☆

Since Nona and I have separate cabins, it's driving me crazy not having someone to tell all my super-secret stuff to. I mean, I'm sitting here on my bunk totally itchy and I can tell my poison oak is rapidly spreading over my entire body. I need to vent to somebody!

I suppose I could talk to one of the girls in my cabin. They seem pretty nice and I think I have them figured out now. Like:

Gabrielle, Gabby for short

"I'm Gabby and I never run out of air and can talk like this for hours and hours and hours . . ."

Her name totally fits her. She talks ninety miles a minute and speaks in run-on sentences without ever taking a breath. I wonder if she's related to my friend Alice. I would love to get the two of them together in a room and sell tickets.

Makayla, aka Insta-Friend

If you talk to her once or give any attention to her, even for a second, she's your instant best friend for life.

Bethanie, aka Super-Happy
(WAY too happy)

For her, the world is made up of rainbows, pink cotton candy, and furry little bunnies. And she totally helps you out in a crisis.

Olivia, aka Rude Girl

Okay, so I still haven't figured out what's up with her. She never looks at us or talks much, and she still kinda seems angry no matter what.

Makayla looks the least distracted, so I go over to talk to her.

She seems to sense gossipy girl talk and flashes a big grin as I approach her. "You're just itching to talk, am I right?"

"You're so right it's almost scary."

So I spill everything, not just about the poison oak, but also about the cute boy who offered me the marshmallows and how Olivia hates me and all my embarrassing moments and . . .

"After having a week like that, we deserve ice cream!" Makayla shouts.

More like a tub full of ice cream!

She says "we" like she shared those moments with me.

"Where do we get ice cream?"

Makayla, being a second-year, tells me about the camp store. She promises to take me there this week during free time, since the store is closed for the day. I need to make sure to tell Nona so she can go with us.

NEWS FLASH

It turns out that using crutches is SUCH a popularity booster.

If I'd known, I would've done something similar during school.

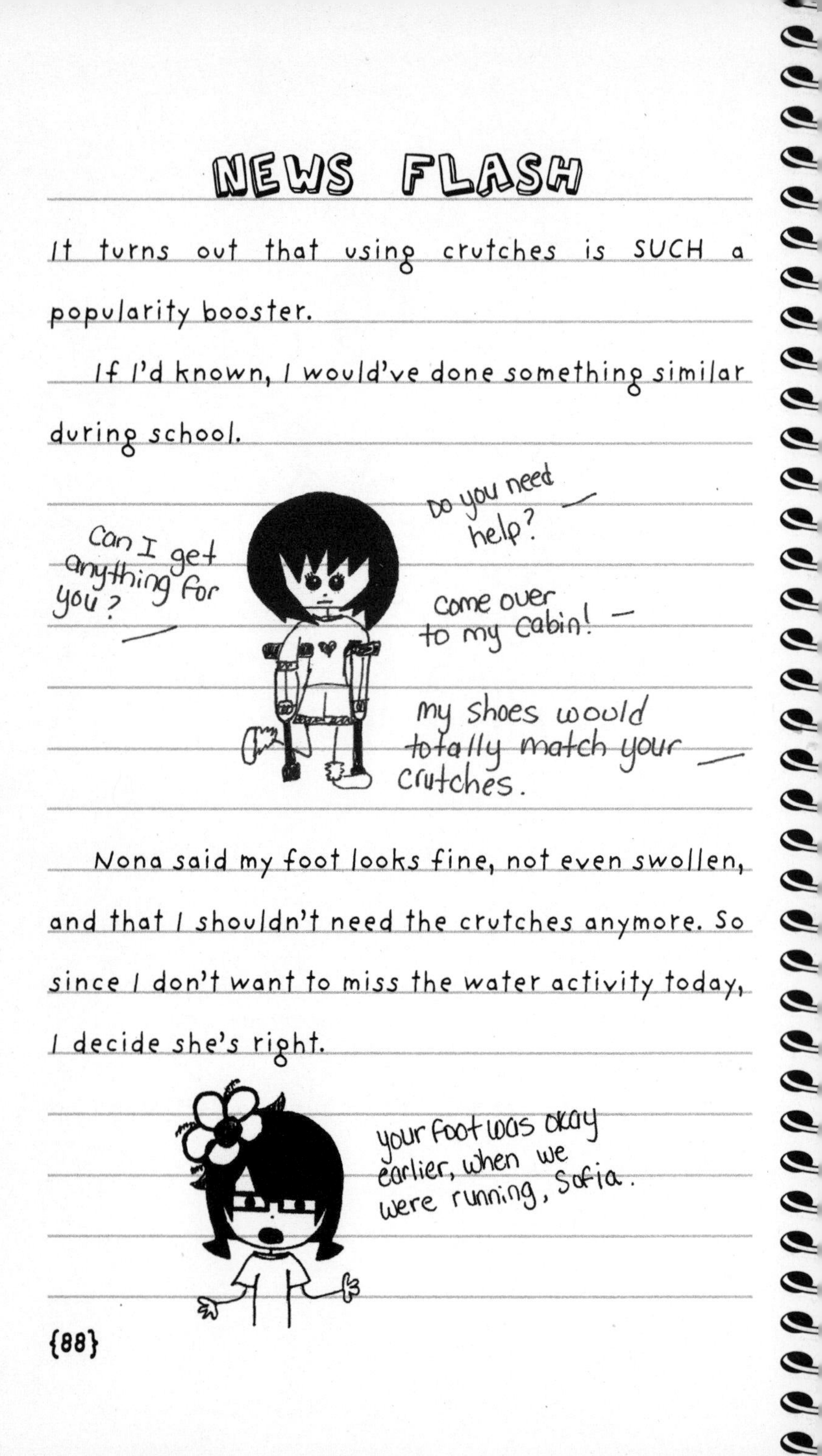

Nona said my foot looks fine, not even swollen, and that I shouldn't need the crutches anymore. So since I don't want to miss the water activity today, I decide she's right.

But then I find out that I don't get to miss the killer hike later on this week. I try to convince The Priss that my ankle is definitely not healed for something that sounds as horrible as that.

Not real bandages.
Bought these online!

Thanks, Nona.

CANOEING

I get so excited when I see the canoes. Not only will a water activity help all my itchiness, but I think it will be totally fun. And I can really convince everyone that I'm a fabulous swimmer and put to rest the rumor that I'm "water disabled."

Plus, I've always, ALWAYS wanted to go canoeing.

It's our cabin and the Monarchs. We line up at the jacket shack to get our life jackets. The counselors talk to us about water safety again and how we must buddy up. Gabby and I pair up and immediately she starts talking excitedly.

And at record-breaking speed.

Gabby hogs the paddles the whole time, so I only get to sit there.

Itching. And listening to Gabby gab. And itching some more.

The Priss makes an announcement as we dry off.

COMPETITION TOMORROW

One team from the Gray Hairstreaks and one from the Monarchs will canoe out to the buoy and back. The first team to finish will be awarded five merits.

The announcement brings out the Monarchs' nasty side. They start talking trash about our cabin, saying how they can row way better than us. It must just be the competitive streak in me, because I find myself blurting out:

The Monarchs just stand there, hands on their hips, like they don't believe me. Okay, so I HAD to tell one little lie. It wasn't my fault; it was my competitive side that decided to blurt it out. It also decided to blurt out something else:

I was canoeing champ at my last camp!

Um, so I guess that's <u>two</u> lies, since I've never been to any other camp before. But still. It makes the Monarch girls back off.

When the whistles blow for us to head back to our cabins, I discover something that was slipped under the door.

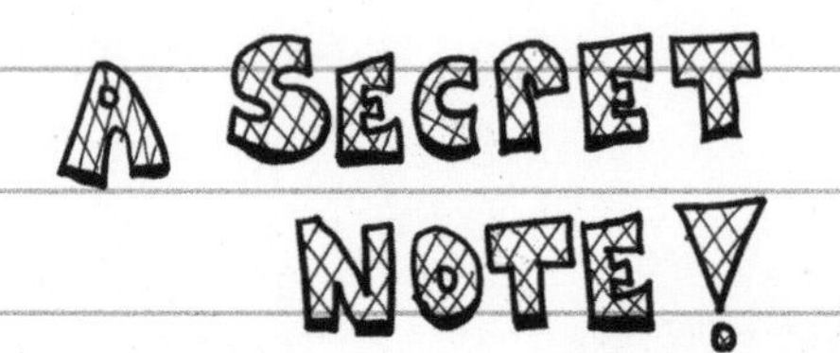

I don't mean to brag, but I'm excellent at analyzing handwriting. One look at the note and I could tell that it was written by some of my fellow campers. Girls who were angry and oozing rivalry.

We don't believe you! We challenge you to a bigger prize for the winners of the canoe challenge. Losers take over chore duty for that day!

– Angry Monarch Girls

I said NO WAY to adding this extra bit of pressure to our challenge, but the other girls in my cabin were all excited and shouted dumb things like:

I guess I had a moment of weakness because I, Sofia Becker, have never been on a team that people actually wanted me to be a part of.

And a bubble of excitement I never felt before convinced me to take on the challenge because somewhere, deep down inside me, there was a canoeing champ ready to be discovered.

I WILL lead our team to Victory!!

I'm so excited I can barely think about anything else.

KILLER HIKE

Any activity with the word "kill" in it should come with protective body gear.

We had to hike forever up windy, narrow paths. On one side of us there was a drop-off cliff. I even threw a rock over the side and didn't hear it land. Looking over the edge really made my feet sweat.

Nona's cabin, the Queens, went with us. So did one of the boys' cabins, the Darklings. Even though I totally hate bugs, that sounds like a really cool beetle!

Other cool names of REAL bugs:

The whole hiking experience was so painful I can barely bring myself to remember all the details. So I won't.

I had my mind on one thing only, so it was hard to concentrate on anything other than canoeing.

Even when Marshmallow Boy smiled at me, I barely remembered to smile back!

CANOE TIME!

It was time to prove myself. To finally fit in with a group simply by being myself (kind of). I started getting nervous when one of the Monarchs came up to me and said:

And then I saw other campers sitting around the lake with binoculars! Well, if they were hoping to catch a close-up of my failure, they were going to be really disappointed.

But then I saw Jackson and Marshmallow Boy sitting down to watch and my heart dropped to my feet. The pressure was on!

Gabby and I were up against two Monarchs named Kendra and Prachi.

Even though I'd never touched a canoe in my life before yesterday, I knew what the oar was for and how I should use it. And really, how hard could it be?

What I didn't realize was how long the oar was and which side I should use to paddle.

So I randomly picked the right side.

I never took my eyes off the oar. I was so focused on my paddling skills and what a natural I seemed to be that I never heard Gabby yelling, "No! Not that way!"

So when our canoe bumped into something, I figured we set a record time reaching the buoy. But as soon as I looked back, I realized we hadn't quite reached the halfway mark.

Actually, it was more like
the starting mark.

Who knew it was possible to row yourself in circles?

We should've stopped there, knowing there was no way we'd win when the Monarchs were rowing back and we were still at the starting point. But

I didn't want to give up, and apparently neither did Gabby, because we both pushed off with our oars and headed back out into the lake. I was so embarrassed but I paddled my heart out anyway. My arms felt like they were about to fall off, so I shouldn't have been surprised when I lost my grip on the oar. Or when it fell into the water. Or when I stupidly tried to grab for it by reaching over the side of the canoe.

At least I tried, right?

This will not be the end for us. I will definitely need to come up with a plan to get us out of chore duty.

THE PLAN

So The Priss wouldn't let us out of chore duty for the Monarchs cabin. Even though they won Messiest Cabin three days in a row. Good thing I had a backup plan!

My plan wasn't like a "Yeah, mopping the floors is fun, let's take lemons and make lemonade!" kind of plan. It was more of a "Let's get even" kind of plan.

This is how it went down.

First we cleaned everything up, and then we had our fun. We snuck over to the bathroom we share with the Monarchs, and Makayla used her clear nail polish on all the bars of soap she could find. Most were inside Ziploc bags in the girls' cubbies, so it wasn't too hard. Now their soap is totally defective, because no matter what they do, they won't be able to make suds. Imagine a cabin full of girls with NO soap!

RANDOM CAMP OBSERVATION

Some valuable camping advice: possums, no matter how cute they are, should not be hand fed. And they don't like trail mix. Oh, and their claws are pretty sharp. Also, canoeing is harder than it looks. Way harder.

SNEAKING A PEEK . . .

I wasn't trying to eavesdrop. I just happened to be standing close enough to Olivia that I could ~~peer~~ glance at her notebook. She writes so much (did I mention way more than me?) that she could probably turn her notebook into a novel.

She was sitting in a beanbag chair in our cabin and was so involved with her notebook that she wasn't paying any attention to me.

From behind her, my eyes swept across the page. She wasn't even writing—she was drawing! And it looked something like this:

So maybe hers is more of a sketchbook, but I didn't have enough time to see more because I started itching like crazy and lost my balance, tripping over my feet and hitting my hand against the wall.

Olivia spun her head around, slamming her notebook shut and glaring at me with this look that was way more intimidating than Nona's meanest look.

Comparison of Mean Looks

"What do you think you're doing?" she said accusingly.

At this point I could do one of two things:

1. Lie and pretend like I was just casually walking by, minding my own business.
2. Be nice and maybe the whole spying thing would be overlooked. Even though I totally was not spying. My eyes just like to . . . wander.

"I love your drawings," I blurted out.

Her look didn't waver, even when I gave her the compliment, so maybe I wasn't being convincing enough.

"I REALLY love your drawings," I said.

Olivia just stared at me, not even cracking a hint of a smile.

"They aren't *drawings,*" she spat out, like there was a bad taste in her mouth.

"Are you sure?" I asked. "Because those really look like drawings."

Olivia scowled. "Yes, I'm SURE they aren't drawings. They are works of art."

A giggle escaped and I clamped a hand over my mouth. Don't get me wrong, her drawings were good. But works of art?

Actually, there are artists out there who throw

paint splotches onto a canvas and get super-famous because of it. So it is a possibility.

Olivia stood up, tucked her notebook under her arm, and angrily stomped away. She muttered something under her breath that sounded like "soup."

RAIN PAINTING

The afternoon activity was painting in the clearing by the lake. It was pretty cool because we weren't allowed to use paintbrushes, only our hands. I painted trees and a mountain, but it could've easily passed as a galaxy.

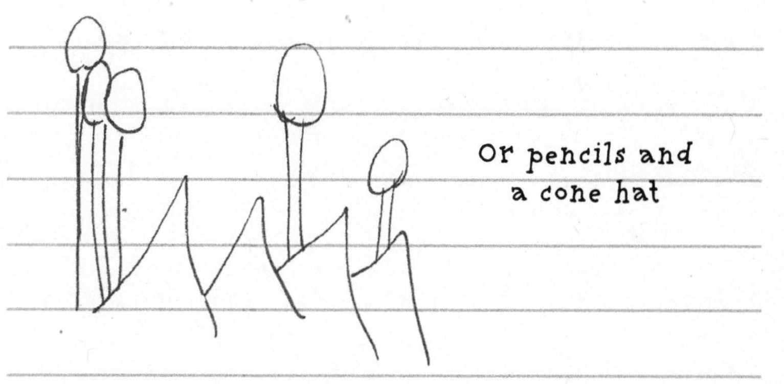

A boy next to me painted a picture of his hands. He was obviously experiencing a creative block.

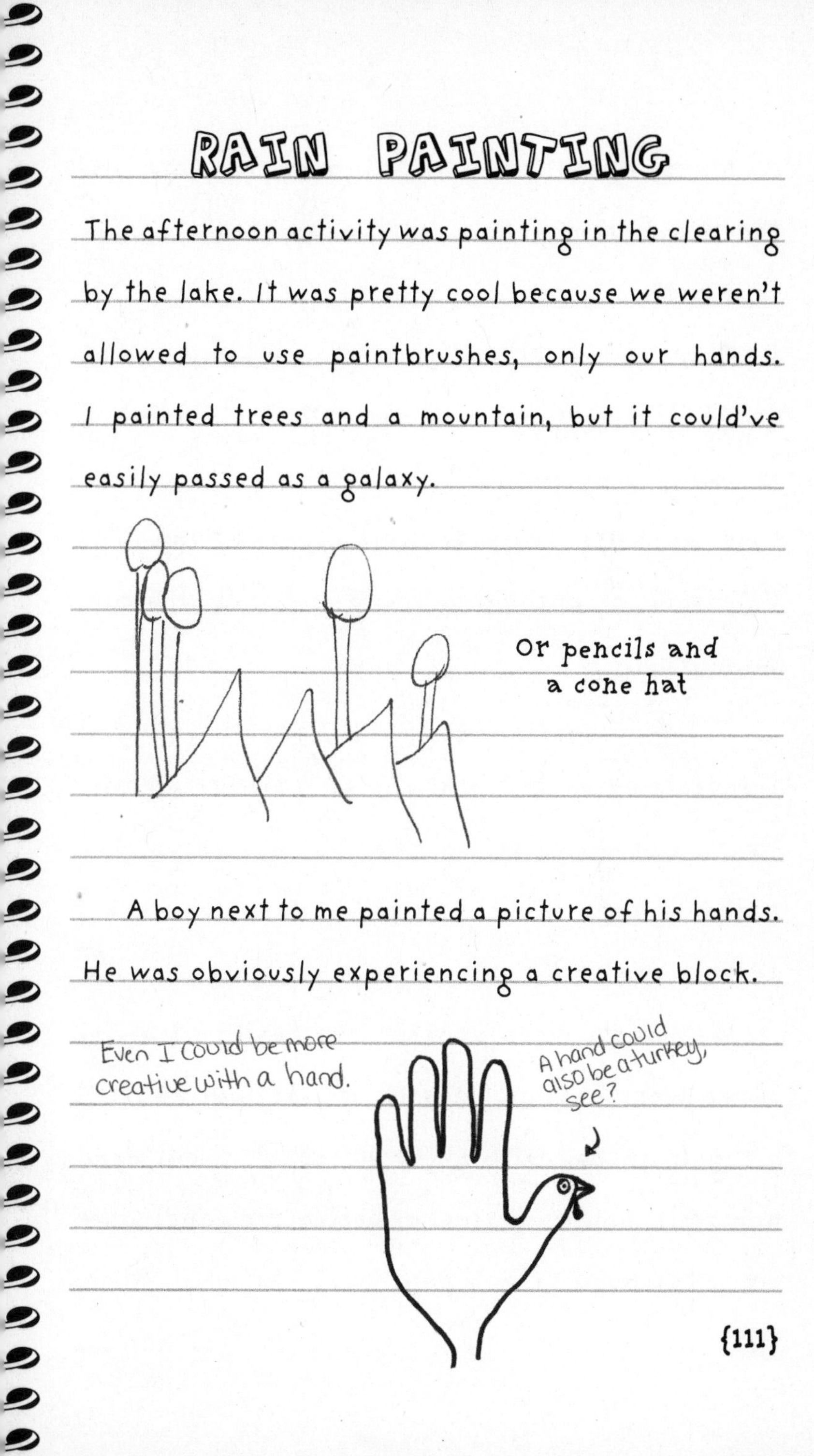

Makayla made splatters all over the page, and the twins from Nona's cabin completed a picture together.

The clouds overhead started sprinkling rain on us. At first everyone was like, "OMG! My painting is going to be ruined!" and "We're getting wet!" Like we were going to melt or something. The CITs said to continue painting and allow the rain to help us.

It was kind of cool to see how our art was transformed so drastically with splatters of rain. Hey, I bet Olivia would like that. I'll forget her rudeness for a minute and tell her about it when I see her again.

We had to wear ponchos the rest of the day if we were outside. Mostly, it was like wearing a big trash bag with holes cut out for your head and arms. And it was just as comfortable. Bethanie wore the hood of her poncho up the whole time, even though it was barely raining. Our ponchos are bright orange, so she kind of looked like a traffic cone.

WHERE'S THE ICE CREAM?

During free-time hour Makayla and I planned our trip up to the camp store. Nona stayed behind so she could play Ping-Pong with the twins. Gabby and Bethanie came with us.

"I want chocolate ice cream. No, wait, I want candy. Yeah, a chocolate candy bar," Makayla said.

The camp store had more than just food. It had stickers and every kind of camping item you might need, like flashlights and batteries.

We ended up each getting an ice cream cone. Since we weren't allowed to bring food into the cabins, we'd have to eat them while walking back.

"I bet I can eat faster than any of you!" Gabby said excitedly.

She's obviously never seen me around food.

"No way!" Bethanie said.

"Okay, then," Makayla said. "First one to eat their entire ice cream cone and be back at the cabin wins!"

It was on!

I'd never eaten ice cream so fast in my life, and I quickly learned that the whole cone wouldn't fit in my mouth.

We were laughing as we ran all the way back to our cabin with ice cream smeared on our faces and dripping down our shirts. Some even ended up in my hair. I got to the cabin door first, but only by a millisecond.

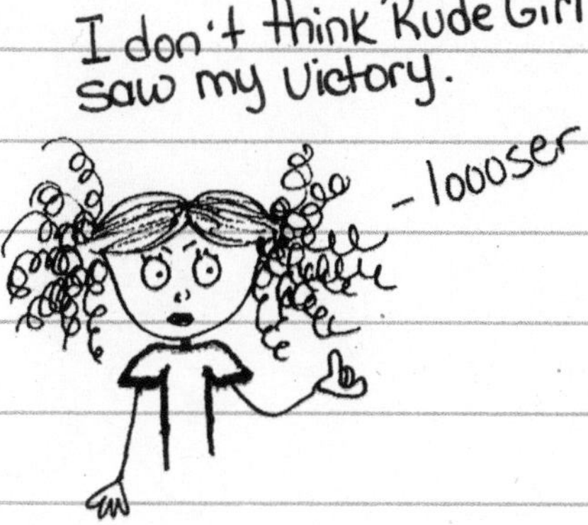
I don't think Rude Girl saw my Victory.
-loooser

We must've been a bigger mess than we realized, because everyone was watching us, laughing. Nona ran up to us with her camera around her neck.

I could totally bribe her with this someday!
say cheese!

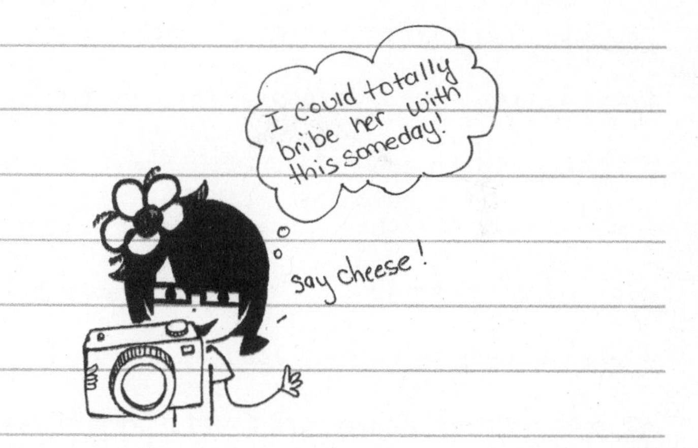

I didn't care who saw us. We were having too much fun. Well, until Marshmallow Boy walked right past us and waved.

☆ ☆ ☆

Okay, so maybe the whole soap prank wasn't such a great idea, because the Monarchs girls fought back. I have to admit, their prank was super-clever. I mean, it would have been if it hadn't happened to us. They must have snuck in while we were sleeping, because this morning when we woke up all sleepy-eyed and stumbling around all zombie-like and still kind of brain-dead, we walked right into their prank.

Literally.

They had covered our doorway with plastic wrap. Where the heck had they gotten that from?

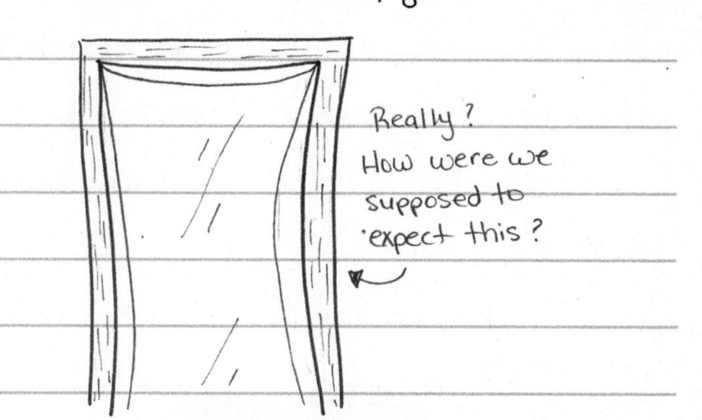

Even though plastic wrap isn't that strong and we weren't walking very fast, it had enough of an impact to cause total chaos.

And once people figured out what was happening, they started pointing fingers.

At me

I don't think I should have to take full blame, because mostly everyone went along with the soap prank. So that's, like, guilty by association or something, right? Or an accessory to a prank?

Makayla, being the new, totally fantastical friend she is, came to my defense.

"Sofia isn't to blame for this," she said.

A girl really needs a friend during a crisis like this.

She was fired up. "Because how can you blame someone who already has a terrific plan to PRANK THEM BACK even better?"

A girl really needs a friend to stop talking during a crisis like this.

So everyone turns to me for my great idea of retaliation and I'm like:

Thanks to Makayla, we are now in the middle of a huge . . .

. . . PRANK WAR!

I'm so not experienced with handling a prank war situation. I only knew that soap trick because I saw it in some movie, so I can't even take full credit for it.

THE PRANK IS ON!

My super-sensitivity to reading people's minds tells me that the Monarchs are expecting us to prank back.

So we will have to do what they did and break

the rules by sneaking into their cabin tonight when everyone is sleeping.

BABY POWDER BLAST

Bethanie has a full bottle of baby powder in her suitcase. Apparently she chafes really badly in the summer.

Other uses for baby powder

BABY Powder

oily hair

BABY Powder

Gets rid of ants

BABY Powder

Hmm...
maybe it will get rid of rude girls too?

So we tiptoe to the other side of the Monarchs cabin, duck beneath the cabin windows, and sneak into the bathroom. Olivia actually participates . . . as the guard. She says she'll whistle if anyone shows up.

I hope she knows how to whistle.

We shake baby powder into each blow dryer inside the cubbies on the Monarchs' side. In the morning, when the girls turn on their dryers, they'll be surprised by a blast of powder. I just wish I could see it!

I would have to say my biggest achievement is not telling Nona any of this secret stuff. All the Gray Hairstreaks swore we wouldn't tell anyone.

RANDOM CAMP OBSERVATION

Pranks can be an awesome way to have fun. It's even more fun when you are way better at it than, say . . . other cabins.

I slept horribly, for a few reasons.

These beds have, like, paper-thin mattresses. Even with my sleeping bag, I think I'm developing back problems like my dad. That thought made me think of my family and I felt a little bit sad. I couldn't believe it, but I actually missed them. Dad's humming. Mom's rules. Halli's crying.

Well, maybe I didn't miss them <u>that</u> much.

I lay awake most of the night in anticipation of the powdery blast this morning. I probably would've slept through the bell if there hadn't been such a commotion outside.

All the girls from the Monarchs cabin were arguing with their CIT and The Priss.

Since most of us slept past shower time (I guess

I wasn't the only exhausted one!), we totally missed how the baby powder blasted into the Monarchs' wet hair and formed some kind of paste.

I have to admit, it sounds totally funny. Way better than we even planned!

Our cabin hurried up and got dressed to go to our first activity. Luckily, The Priss didn't mention anything to us about the prank. But I'm sure she knew it was us.

She probably even has it written down on her clipboard.

Anything that goes wrong is Sofia's fault.

My girls pranked the Monarchs, which means Sofia is behind it.

The afternoon activity is making ice cream. I can tell I'll be a pro at this.

I don't think it's possible to ever have too much ice cream. So I'm super-excited, but the only person I know in my group is Olivia. Jonah, one of the counselors from the boys' cabin, pairs us up. I was hoping my partner would be some cute boy, but of course I get Olivia, since we're standing next to each other. She scowls at me as soon as Jonah says my name.

I give her my best scowl back.

Each team gets two clear plastic bags. One large and one medium. The counselor passes out instruction cards and tells us to get started. All the ingredients are on the tables in front of us.

This should be a piece of cake. I won't even need to talk to Olivia.

I hold the large bag open with both hands while Olivia fills it up with ice and rock salt. Then she stands there staring at me.

"Zip it!" she says angrily.

"What? I didn't say anything."

Olivia rolls her eyes. "Zip. The. Bag."

Geez, could she be any ruder?

I close the bag, then hold open the medium-sized one while Olivia fills it with the rest of the ingredients. We seal it, place it inside the large bag, and start shaking.

Honestly, I don't even know why we need two people for this.

24 SECONDS LATER . . .

OMG! My arms are going to fall off!

Olivia smirks. "Whatever. But we have to shake this bag for a full five minutes."

I hand the bag to Olivia. Since she thinks it's so easy, she can do it for the rest of the time. She calls me a wuss under her breath before wimping out herself only a minute later. She actually laughs then, calling us "total wimps with weak arms." We go back and forth like this until our timer dings.

The best part was making a sundae out of the whole mess. The counselors gave us a ton of different toppings to choose from. The ice cream itself was super-tasty, even though it didn't make a whole lot. But it was SUPER-cold.

I got brain freeze just looking at it.

Really, we only made, like, one scoop of ice cream. I think it's much easier to just buy ice cream from the store. But in case I ever want to relive this experience again (not), I taped the recipe card into my notebook to save.

What You'll Need

- 1 tablespoon sugar
- 1/2 cup milk or half & half
- 1/4 teaspoon vanilla
- 6 tablespoons rock salt
- 1 pint-size plastic food storage bag (e.g., Ziploc)
- 1 gallon-size plastic food storage bag
- Ice cubes

How To Make It

Fill the large bag half full of ice, and add the rock salt. Seal the bag. Put milk, vanilla, and sugar into the small bag, and seal it. Place the small bag inside the large one, and seal it again. Shake until the mixture is ice cream, which takes about 5 minutes. Wipe off the top of the small bag, then open it carefully. Enjoy!

LIGHTS-OUT!

I was so exhausted by the time it was lights-out that I fell asleep the moment my head hit the pillow. Our cabin does pretty well with following the rules at night. Actually, most of the merit points we earn are for Quietest Cabin During Lights-Out.

So of course I'm the one to break a rule first. Actually, three rules. Honestly, it takes someone truly skillful to break three rules at one time.

So tonight while I was innocently sleeping, I was attacked in my sleep. By bugs. Okay, not just bugs. Something much, much worse than that. Black moths. I woke up to the feeling of something hitting me. And since they blended so perfectly into the darkness, I thought at first that I was imagining things. Or that maybe I was still asleep.

But after one got tangled in my hair, I jumped out of my bunk, screaming. And, if I remember right, hyperventilating. I grabbed my flashlight from underneath my pillow and turned it on to see a mob of moths surrounding me.

Oh, yeah, AND they're attracted to light.

Of course I woke up the whole cabin.

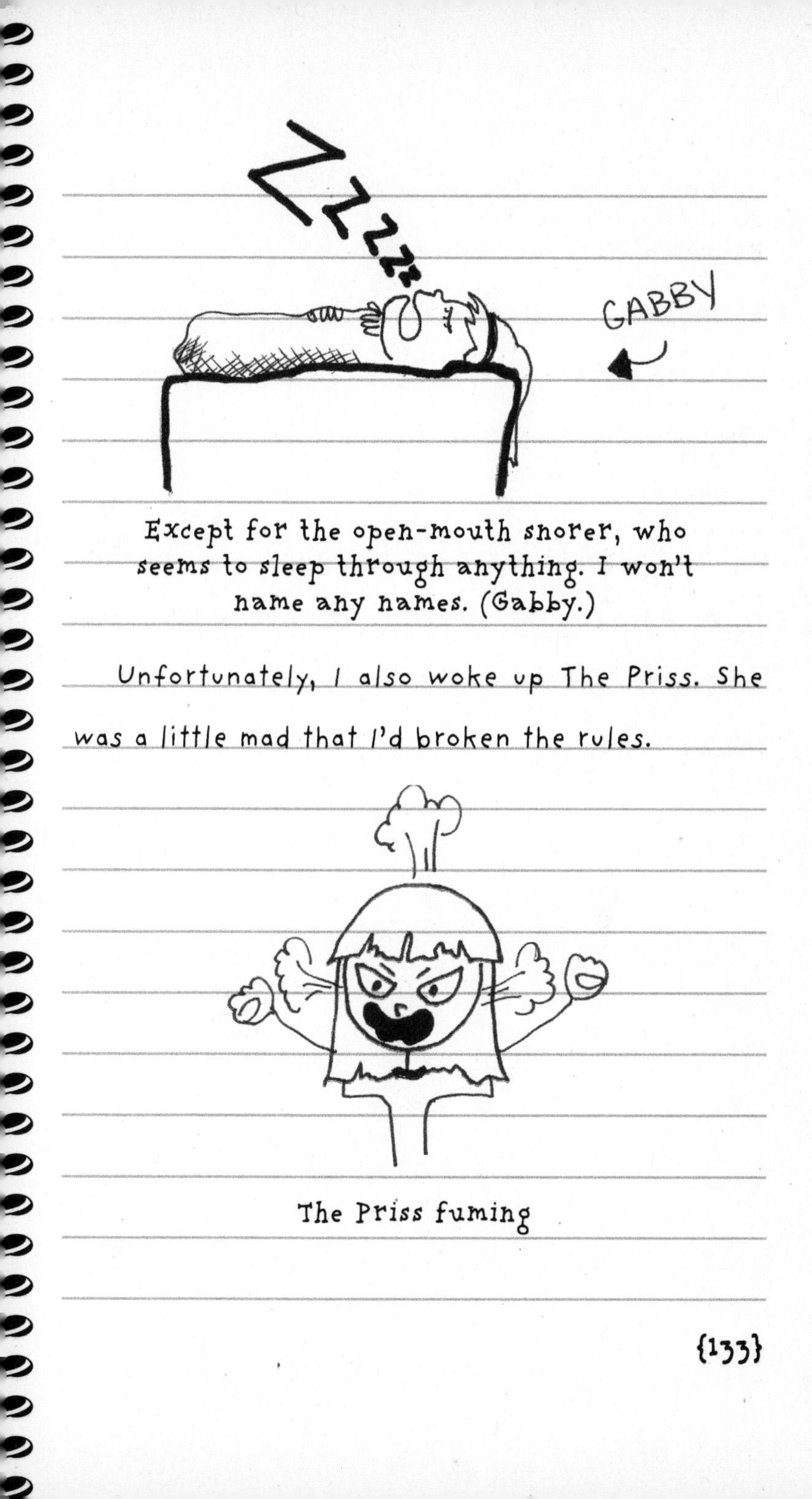

Except for the open-mouth snorer, who seems to sleep through anything. I won't name any names. (Gabby.)

Unfortunately, I also woke up The Priss. She was a little mad that I'd broken the rules.

The Priss fuming

And for every rule we break, we get a point deducted from our cabin total. So I was responsible for demoting our cabin from first to third place.

Some might have considered my situation an emergency, which means two rules were broken, not three.

But I'm sure we can recover some of our points if we have the quietest and straightest line the next time we head to the dining hall.

NEW DAY, NEW CRUSH

So I'm feeling kind of guilty about having a new crush. And to make matters even more complicated, while we were sitting in the dining hall, Nona noticed a boy looking at me.

He's sitting 6 tables . . .
no, 8 tables up. And
4 people from the
right. It's so obvious!

When I went to look, Nona said, "Don't look! You'll make it way too obvious!"

So I never actually saw the boy. But Nona assured me that he was looking at ME, the way someone does when they are crushing on you.

So since he's crushing on me, that means he should probably be my crush too.

How you know when you have a crush:

1. You think about him. A LOT.
2. Your stomach feels like it's tied in double knots with a really big rope.
3. You can't wait to see him.

So far, numbers 1 and 3 apply to the mystery boy. I mean, I've been thinking about him nonstop since Nona said he was looking at me. I wonder who he is. And it's true, I can't wait to see him. Because Nona is the only one who's seen him so far. I'm pretty sure the reason my stomach doesn't feel tied in knots yet is because I don't know what he looks like. But if I'm crushing on him, I'm pretty sure that will change soon. Plus, I'm kinda crushing on Marshmallow Boy too.

I'm pretty much a crush magnet.

Nona promised to point out Mystery Boy (discreetly) to me the next time he's close by.

CONFESSION

I feel a little guilty for having another crush. Or two. You might think I shouldn't crush on anyone else while I'm crushing on my biggest crush ever, Andrew. The rules for having more than one crush:

1. You must be faithful to your longest crush.
2. You can have a crush on someone else, but it must be a smaller crush than the one you have on your longest crush. (See rule #1.)
3. Your second crush doesn't really count if it's only temporary (like four weeks).
4. Or if it's in another zip code.
5. Or if your first crush doesn't even know about your second crush. Or your third.

So really, I'm not breaking any of the crush rules. Also, Nona says that whatever happens at Crack-A-Toe stays at Crack-A-Toe. Except for everything I'm writing in my notebook.

Oh, no! Oh, no! Remember that doodle note Nona and I made out of boredom during that video? IT. IS. GONE. I had it tucked away in my notebook, but I just realized it's not here! It must've fallen out.

If it fell out, it could be anywhere. Where anyone could read it! This is not good. This is SO not good.

STINK-OUT!

Today, some girl got sprayed by a skunk while on a hike. Apparently, she still smells pretty terrible, even after showering and using tomato juice and her fruity shampoos.

FREE-TIME HOUR

I spotted Olivia sitting by herself on a rock by the lake. I kinda felt bad for her because she's usually alone, but I figured that's how she wants it. But I know what it's like to sit alone (when Nona isn't at school) and what it feels like to not belong, knowing that people are talking about you behind your back.

Three sides to a rude girl

somewhat rude

mostly rude

way rude

But we only said things about her like how she was being mean, so that doesn't really count.

I walked up to her and she slammed her notebook shut the minute she saw me.

"Don't worry, I don't want to see," I assured her.

"Good," she said.

"I just wanted to say I'm sorry," I said.

"Why?" she asked, still acting all defensive.

"Just because, you know, I'm sorry for snooping."

She didn't say anything, just looked kind of surprised. I turned around and headed back to camp, smiling to myself. She wasn't as mean as she pretended to be.

ITCHING TO FIND OUT!

I passed Jackson on the way back to camp and got up the guts to ask him about his poison oak.

He looked at me kind of weird. "Uh, I never had poison oak."

I was so embarrassed that I quickly fled, even though he was about to say something else.

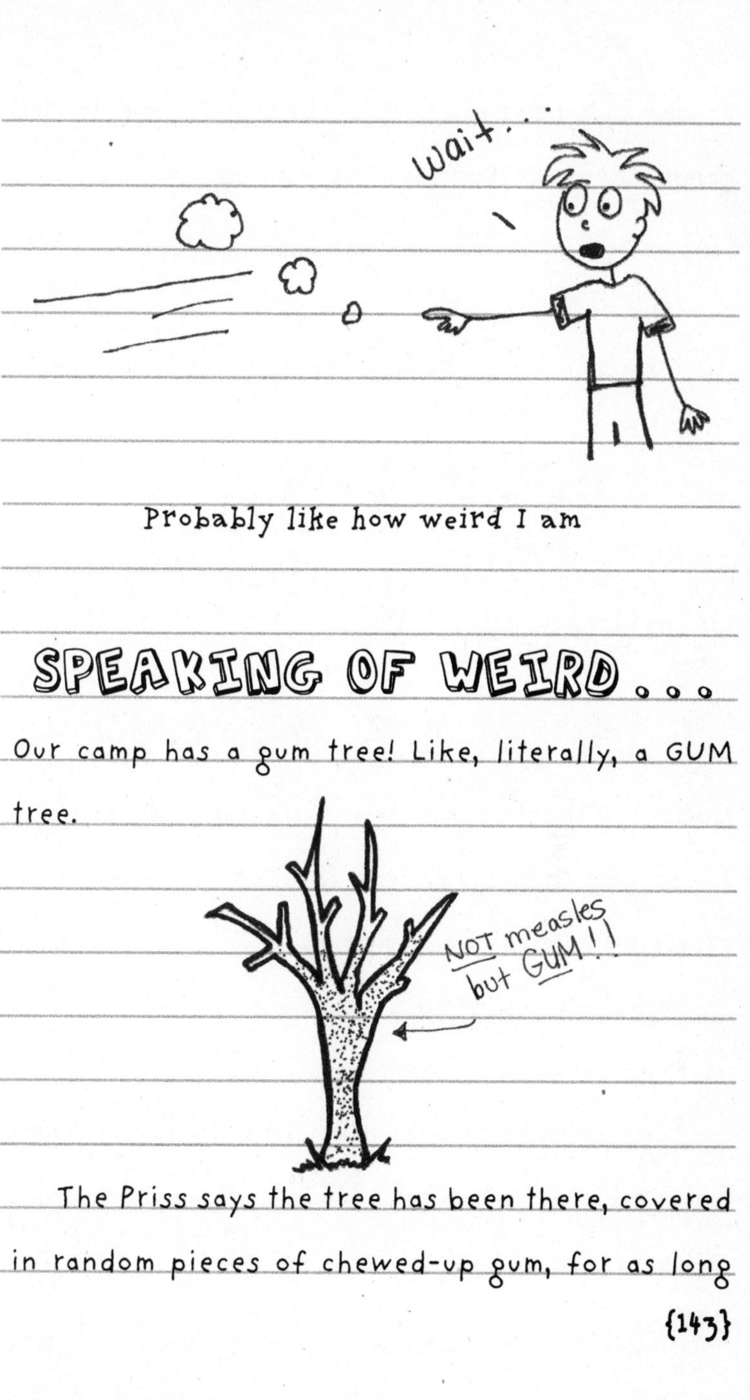

Probably like how weird I am

SPEAKING OF WEIRD . . .

Our camp has a gum tree! Like, literally, a GUM tree.

The Priss says the tree has been there, covered in random pieces of chewed-up gum, for as long as she can remember. And she first came to this camp when she was eight years old!

Yuck!

TOTALLY RANDOM

Nona approaches me and tells me how the guy I was just talking to was the same one who was staring at me in the dining hall.

"Who? Jackson?" I asked.

"Yep."

"Yeah, right, Nona! He doesn't like me. He was only staring at me because HE was the one I embarrassed myself in front of that one day. You know, when he gave me the sumac paper towels. He probably thinks I'm weird. Oh, yeah, and he never even had poison oak. What a liar!"

BACK IN THE DINING HALL . . .

Nona says Jackson is staring at me again, but I don't believe her.

"You're imagining things," I say.

"No, I'm not. He's right there!"

"Where?" I ask.

She nods toward where he's sitting, and yes, he

_is_ looking in my direction! Then he kind of nods and gives me a quick smile.

I lift my hand to wave. The same hand that's holding the fork I'm eating my mashed potatoes with. Before I even have a chance to realize it, my potatoes fling off my fork and land in the hair of a girl sitting directly across from me one table over.

This is NOT my fault for two reasons:

1. They gave us forks to eat our mashed potatoes with. Everyone knows you need a spoon.
2. The mashed potatoes aren't thick. They are actually kinda runny, which makes it way too easy to accidentally fling them across the dining hall. It's like the dining hall people are just begging us to start a food fight.

The girl turns around. It's some snobby girl from the Monarchs named Elizabeth-Libby. And somehow, she knows I was the cause of the lump of potatoes stuck in her hair.

"Sorry!" I yell to Elizabeth-Libby. "My fork is totally faulty!"

She doesn't say anything. She simply picks a piece of bread off her plate and flings it. I'm guessing she was aiming for me, but bread doesn't fly across the room as well as mashed potatoes, so it falls short.

And ends up smacking Nona in the head

Before I can stop her, Nona sends a ton of mushy baby carrots soaring toward Elizabeth-Libby, but she ends up hitting, like, twenty different people instead.

I probably don't have to say what came next, since it's so predictable, but I will anyway.

FOOD FIGHT!

And I do the only thing I can think of.

I hide under the table.

We also lost about a bazillion merits, so we're probably in the negative points now.

MYSTERY CABIN

During Campfire Friday, this girl Emily tells us a story about the cabin across the lake. I never really noticed it before because it's hidden behind trees, so unless you know it's there, it's kind of hard to see.

She continues, "Nobody knows who visits the cabin. But rumor has it, a monster lives there."

Emily goes on. "But a few people have dared to venture close enough to it, and when they

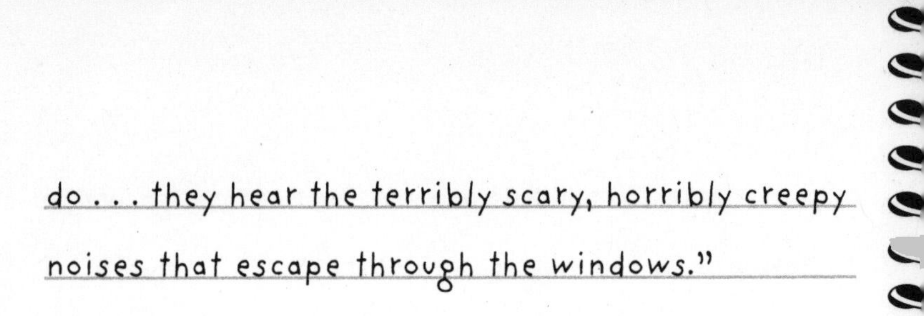

do . . . they hear the terribly scary, horribly creepy noises that escape through the windows."

Emily clears her throat, a little irritated with all the interruptions. "So nobody knows for sure who, or what, lives there."

And then she stops. Everyone waits for her to say more, to get to the good part, but she doesn't. Instead, when someone asks what REALLY is in that cabin, Emily shrugs and says, "I don't know. It's not a ghost story. It's just true."

Well, in my opinion, that is the most horrible true ghost story I've ever heard.

TALES FROM THE TWILIGHT TRAILS

One of the most disappointing days ever. I was totally amped up for the twilight hike. Bethanie and I were playing this game where you close your eyes and try to walk in a straight line. It's actually pretty fun because for some reason, you really can't walk in a straight line when your eyes are closed. When it was my turn, the trail curved but I managed to walk straight.

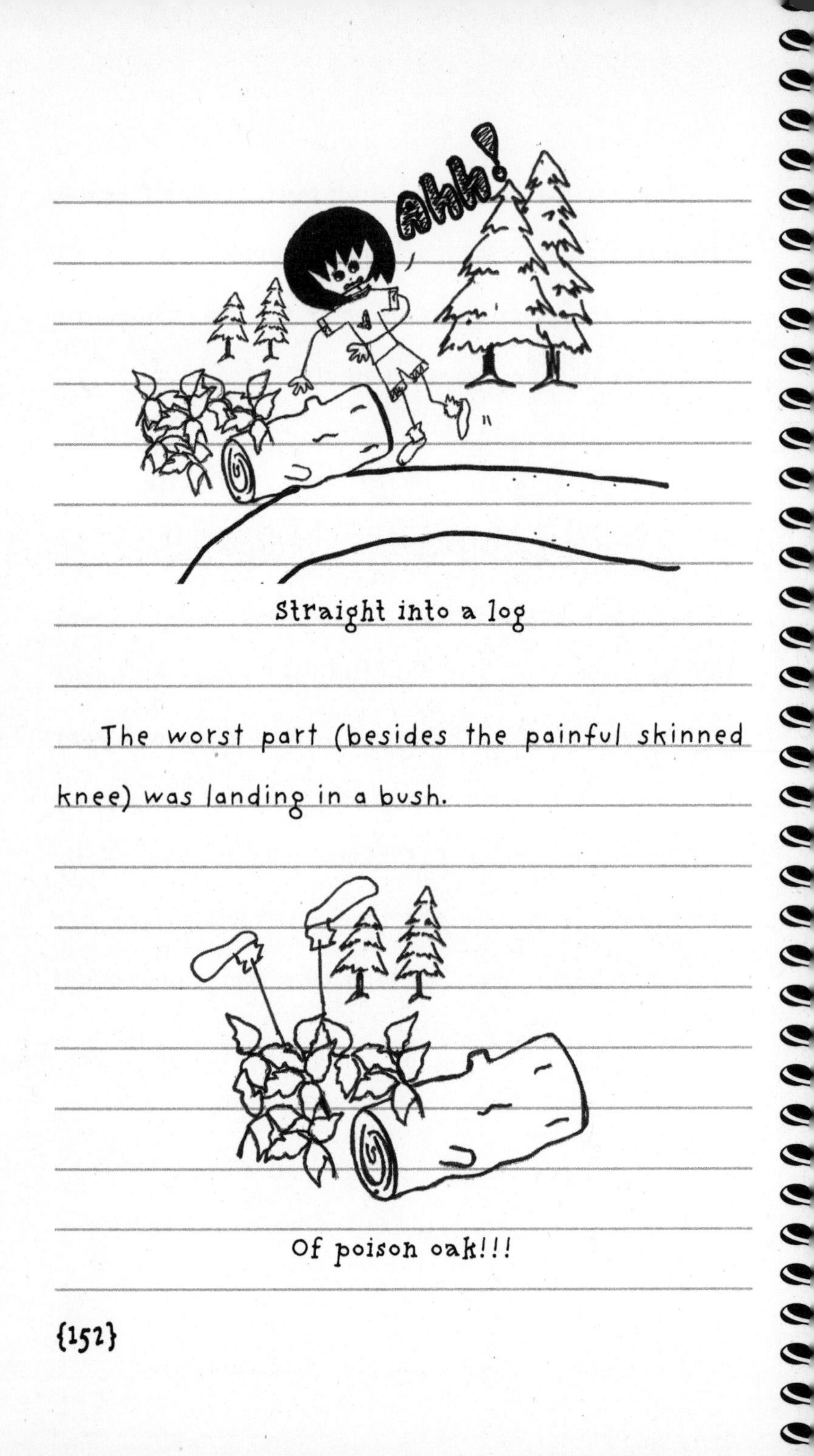

Straight into a log

The worst part (besides the painful skinned knee) was landing in a bush.

Of poison oak!!!

And the twilight hike had absolutely NOTHING to do with vampires. Sigh.

GLOW-IN-THE-DARK FUN!

Tonight we're playing glow-in-the-dark Frisbee!

All the camp Frisbees glow in the dark, but the counselors have added some extra "glowiness" for fun.

We get to wear glow-stick necklaces. And bracelets.

I think we're more excited about the glowing than the actual game.

The CITs have us scatter out randomly so that we're mixed in with campers from other cabins. Which wouldn't be so bad if Nona was with me.

Playing glow-in-the-dark Frisbee is much harder than it actually sounds, for several reasons:

1. There are too many trees. It's easy to confuse them for actual people.

2. People don't play fair. Some people are total Frisbee hogs and rarely toss the Frisbee to you. So you stand there, not really paying attention, and . . . SMACK! You get a Frisbee to the head.

Or ten.

3. People cheat. Like really, how do you cheat at Frisbee, right? Some of the boys thought it would be fun to hide their glow sticks and sneak up on the rest of us unsuspecting campers and steal the Frisbees from us.
4. People don't play by the rules. Okay, so there aren't really any "rules" if you want to get all technical, but there should be. I mean, did you realize how many ways you can get bruises from playing this game?

But other than that, it was a way fun game and a perfect excuse to "accidentally" run into cute boys.

I have it! An idea, that is. I just quietly told all the Gray Hairstreaks (ugh, I still hate that name) to ~~bring~~ sneak their glow-in-the-dark items back to the cabin and I'll explain our next prank.

THAT NIGHT . . .

We snuck over to the Monarchs cabin while everyone was sleeping and opened up our glowy items with scissors that we kind of "borrowed" from the art center. We dripped the glow stuff from inside the bracelets and necklaces all over the Monarchs' arms.

THEN . . .

We all went back to our cabin, except for Bethanie. She went up to the oak tree and rang the camp bell! Then she fled to the restrooms and hid.

We peeked out our window as everyone in camp ran outside. All the Monarchs had glowing spots on their arms.

I guess we should've run outside too, because everyone instantly guessed we were the ones behind it since we were the only cabin pretending to be asleep.

MORNING TIME!

After breakfast, when we went back to our cabin, we couldn't open the door. Our hands kept slipping off the doorknob. It was like trying to turn the knob with wet hands. Except our hands weren't wet.

The Priss shoved past us and said, "Okay, girls, enough playing around. Let's just go in." But when she tried the knob, her hand slid right off too. She looked down at it, then at us.

"What did you girls do now?"

What she really meant:

Really? Does she have to talk to us like we're troublemakers?

Like it was our fault the knob was acting all weird or something.

The Priss held up her hands. "Really? Vaseline?"

We all said "Ohhhhh" in a hushed tone until she finally got that it really wasn't our fault and we had been totally pranked.

When we finally got the door open, The Priss just about fell as she slid across the floor, grabbing for the wall. Either someone intentionally Vaselined the floors or they just made a mess, we're not sure. But still, someone could have really hurt themselves.

DOUBLE PRANK!

Plus, seriously? Isn't there some sort of rule about pranking twice in one day?

Wait a second . . . *I* brought Vaseline to camp.

Wait another second . . . What are the chances that someone else did too?

"You know what this means, right, girls?" The Priss asked us, clasping her clipboard. She and Khloe exchanged glances.

What? More merit points deducted? An early lights-out? No ONE cookie before bed?

If there was ever a time our cabin felt like a team, it was now. And for once, The Priss used her clipboard for something totally useful: to write down ideas for the biggest prank in the history of all Crack-A-Toe pranks. Ever.

While everyone was busy talking, I looked in my suitcase, and just as I expected, my Vaseline was gone.

So we got pranked with our own stuff. And I suspect I know exactly who stole my Vaseline.

I will need to have
a serious talk with Nona.

But what I don't understand is how Nona got involved in any of this.

RANDOM CAMP OBSERVATION

It's never cool to steal things from people. Even if they are your best friend. And on a side note, I'm pretty sure I got poison oak. I can feel it making me itchy.

BIGFOOT BASH!

Tonight is a secret Bigfoot bash. We will sneak out of our sleeping bags when we're sure the CITs are asleep. We have a hush-hush meeting spot, and Emily from the Monarchs cabin has a digital camera to capture any evidence. It was Nona's idea to bring Emily along. She swears we can trust her, but I'm going to still keep an eye on her. We've set a trap that is likely to entice the Bigfoot to our area. But don't worry, we have sticks to protect ourselves.

And running shoes for a quick getaway

11:00 p.m. No sign of any hairy apelike beasts. Although there was a loud boom, but Olivia said that was just Emily sneezing. I still have to wonder.

11:05 p.m. Another booming noise. It is, in fact, Emily sneezing. Her sneezes seem unnaturally loud. Maybe we could use them as weapons too, if she knows how to sneeze on command.

11:20 p.m. There was a bright light that flickered in our direction! I doubt Bigfoot carries a flashlight, but Bethanie is convinced we're in for an alien invasion.

11:21 p.m. A HORRIBLE smell. Like a decaying animal. It's so bad we stuff toilet paper up our nostrils. But then we have to breathe through our mouths and we can taste the horribleness.

11:22 p.m. That smell was just Nona airing out her feet. We got all excited over the smelly horribleness for nothing! So disappointing.

11:30 p.m. We're back in our sleeping bags. We were totally busted. That bright light was a flashlight, but it was CIT Jay from the boys' cabin. How did he know we were out there? Someone must've ratted on us. Yes, I definitely smell a rat. (And might I add, a rat smells more pleasant than Nona's feet!)

BATHROOM BUDDIES

Okay, so we're not SUPPOSED to go anywhere at night without a buddy. My problem is I have to use the bathroom, and my buddy—Makayla—sleeps like a log. Or a rock. She will not wake up.

And really, I don't want to wake up any of the other girls, because it will probably only make them mad. So what will it hurt if I run to the bathroom by myself?

I remind myself it's not that far as I walk quickly through the darkness with only my flashlight, which doesn't provide much comfort. Especially with hairy beasts running around.

A HORRIBLE NOISE!

It sounds like a kid screaming. Or my dad's singing. I shine my flashlight in the direction of the noise and I see . . . that I'm not alone.

No bears. Or raccoons. Or mountain lions. Or even Bigfoot. But a different kind of dangerous animal that the camp counselors failed to mention to us.

Filthy Stray Cats

But not just any dirty stray cats. I'm pretty certain these cats are rabid! They're making low, throaty growls, their eyes are glowing like UFOs, and they're surrounding the entrance to the bathroom. This brings back memories.

Cats don't just hate water.
They hate, HATE water.

Aha! That's what I need to do! No, not give them baths, but spray them with water. Except I don't have a spray bottle with me. Or water. BUT . . . I have my pineapple spray. And it must be good for something other than attracting mosquitoes. I run back to my cabin and quickly grab it.

Yes, I am now armed with pineapple spray.

I go back and get only as close to the cats as I need to.

Okay, so cats apparently hate fruit spray even more than water. Instead of scattering, they got super-angry. Because they ran. Toward me!

I nearly lost my life!

And to make things even worse, I ran so quickly that I ended up in the wrong cabin. I walked right into the Queens'. I snuck out of there just as quickly, though, so hopefully nobody saw me.

RANDOM CAMP OBSERVATION

Things I've learned: Never walk outside at night by yourself. And never spray a cat with ANYTHING. There's nothing worse than a mad cat. Actually, there is. Ten mad cats. But let's forget I mentioned this.

THE VERY NEXT DAY

I can't wait for Campfire Friday. I have a wicked awesome story to share that will knock everyone's socks off.

The inspiration for my story hit me like a sleeping bag of bricks.

This will be my chance to show everyone my unbelievable storytelling skills. And show off my creative brain too. It's so super-secret that I haven't even told Nona my story. I told her I could only give her a few hints.

TRUTH OR LIE?

So we got together as a cabin and played Two Truths and a Lie. The rules are simple: Each person tells three things about themselves, and one is a lie. Everyone has to guess which one. Olivia was by far the easiest to figure out.

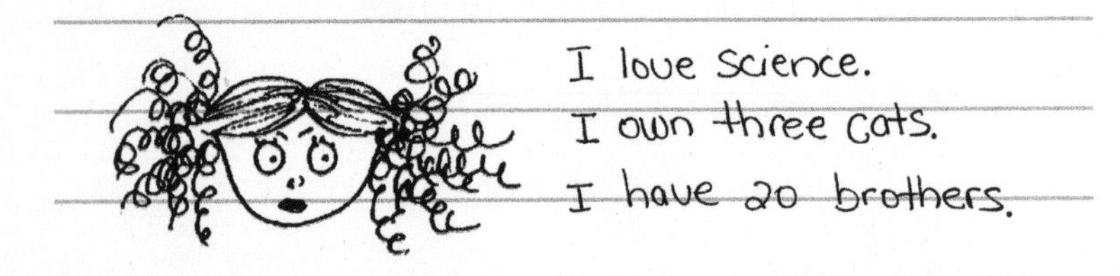

With Gabby, it was a little harder to guess the lie.

IOnceWonAWritingContest.
ICollectHats.
I'mAfraidOfAllReptiles.

Even The Priss and Khloe played.

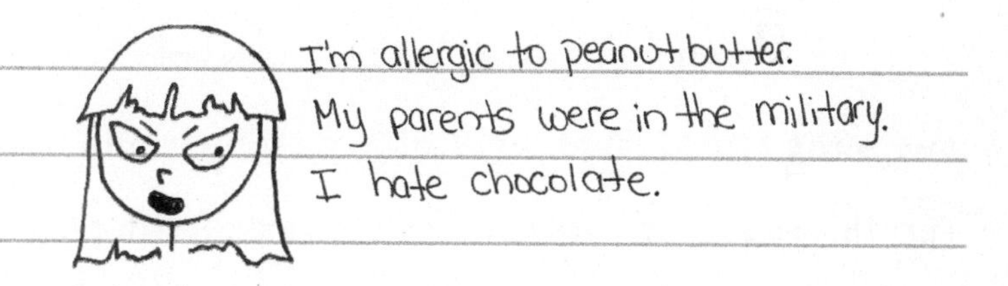

Turns out The Priss's parents really were in the military. Maybe that's why she's so super-strict and a natural whistle blower.

Then it was my turn.

I love chocolate.
I'm a secret blogger.
I once met a famous person.

So Olivia has to break the rules of the game and shouts:

I can feel my face getting bright red as everyone starts laughing. I bite my tongue and wait for Olivia's next turn so I can think of something twice, no, FOUR times as clever to say about her! But then I realize a better way to get back at her.

Everyone kind of looks at me like they're expecting me to yell at her or be completely angry, but instead, I walk calmly over to my bunk and snatch up the glow-in-the-dark friendship bracelets that came in my care package. I give each girl a bracelet, Olivia first.

She just looks at me like she's stunned.

"Why are you giving me this?" she asks.

"I'm giving a bracelet to everyone here because you guys are my friends," I say.

I even hand one to Khloe and to The Priss, and they both give me actual, happy smiles.

Then I say, "Why else?" and roll my eyes. I can't have her thinking I'm too nice.

SPOOKY STORY TIME!

So tonight I get to tell my story. I can hardly wait. I can tell the other girls are just as excited, if not more!

Everyone leans in as I tell the story in a low, hushed voice. I put the flashlight under my chin like people do in the movies to give my face that extra-creepy look.

"A man named Mr. Jones was walking down a totally quiet road super-late at night," I begin. "He heard a knocking . . . wait, no . . . he heard a rapping noise. Being the way-curious person he is, he followed the noise to an old, creepy house."

"The rapping noise grew louder. And louder. Mr. Jones really didn't want to go inside that creepy old house. I mean, it looked like something out of a ghost story. The super-spooky kind. But he just had to know what was causing the noise. So he approached the house and slowly turned the knob on the front door. The rapping noise grew louder and louder. Mr. Jones followed the noise and crept up the creaky stairs, where the rapping was even louder! His heart practically thudded right out of his chest. But Mr. Jones wasn't all that smart, because he still continued to follow the rapping noise . . . up to the attic."

"The noise was so loud he nearly had to cover his ears. He opened the door to the attic, and inside was a dusty antique trunk. The rapping noise was coming from inside the trunk. Shaking with fear, Mr. Jones fumbled with the lock and quickly threw open the lid."

I lower my voice even more and say the next part in a whisper.

"And guess what he found inside?"

"Okay, wait for it. Wait for it." Long pause. "It was rapping paper!"

I totally wasn't expecting THIS kind of reaction. Where was the laughter? Where were the bone-chilling shivers?

And then they threw marshmallows at me. The Priss didn't even stop them!

In fact, I think she threw some at me too!

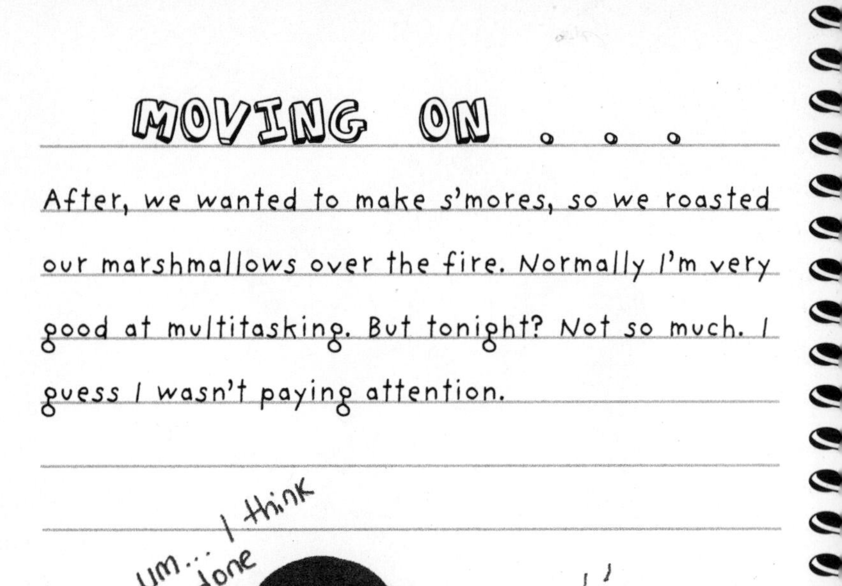

MOVING ON . . .

After, we wanted to make s'mores, so we roasted our marshmallows over the fire. Normally I'm very good at multitasking. But tonight? Not so much. I guess I wasn't paying attention.

Anytime something catches fire, I kinda maybe freak out, ever since that one time Nona and I tried to give a dirty kitty a bath (her idea) and light candles (also her idea) and the whole bathroom caught fire.

So I start blowing frantically on my marshmallow.

Blowing on it was a bad idea. Because it made the flame bigger. And it kind of sort of jumped onto the hair of the girl next to me.

But it only singed the ends. So really, it wasn't as bad as everyone made it seem.

I even offered to cut the burnt ends of her hair for her, you know, to say I was sorry.

But she just screamed and ran from me.

PRANK PLAN

We've been totally scheming and NOT pranking. On purpose. The first part of our prank plan was not to prank. It makes total sense. We wait until the Monarchs think we've given up, and at the last moment, when they least expect it, we strike.

Like a snake.

Our plan involves sneaking into the kitchen late at night, after everyone is asleep. Khloe has a key and will "accidentally drop it" by Olivia's bunk. Then we will all conveniently slip out and grab the "ingredients" on our list. Just like the Monarchs, we found out, snuck into the kitchen when they used plastic wrap on our doorway.

RECIPE FOR DISASTER

1. Whipped cream
2. Peanut butter
3. Jell-O powder
4. Eggs
5. Any canned food item

PRANK DAY!

So our prank is called the Foodie Goodie. And it's actually a whole bunch of pranks at one time. Each of us is assigned to one prank.

The Priss took a can of baked beans and used it to prop open the door to the Monarchs cabin. That way we could sneak in and out easily without making much noise. She motioned with her hand for us to go.

Olivia grabbed a jar of peanut butter and snuck in first. She was going to put a bit of peanut butter on the hands of the sleeping Monarchs. Hopefully they would be in a position where she could do this to most of them. It took her longer than we thought, but as she squeezed back out the door, she crouched down while running back, telling the next person to go.

Bethanie went next, carrying a carton of eggs. Her job was to place an egg in every shoe she could find next to the girls' bunks.

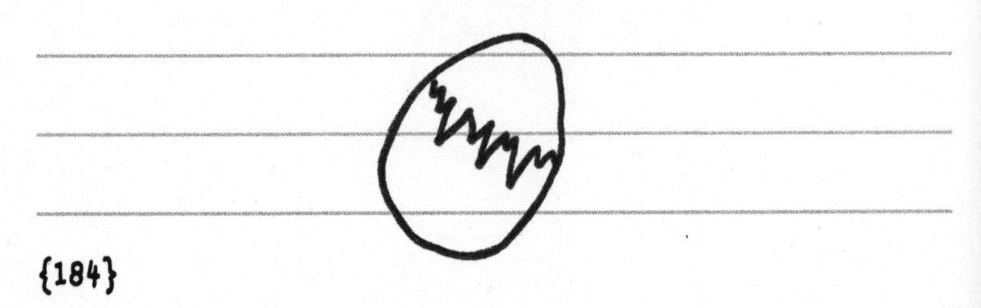

"Go, Makayla!" I whispered as I saw Bethanie on her way back.

We all had our heads poked out of our cabin door, watching each girl one by one complete her task.

Makayla had put three cans of whipped cream in the freezer yesterday. Tonight she was going to place each can in a sock (to disguise the coldness) and tuck the socks in three different girls' sleeping bags.

As soon as she was done, Gabby and I headed over together, since we were the last ones. I was in charge of putting Jell-O powder mix in the girls' sleeping bags while Gabby put in water balloons.

And then we all went back inside our cabin to laugh.

IT WAS TIME!

It was an hour later. We all rushed to the tree with the bell. We tugged on the rope, making it clang as loud and as long as possible. We knew we were going to get caught, but that was the point.

I'm sure the Monarchs were completely startled awake, because we heard some groans and grumbles and someone yelling out, "What's going on?" But because they were still half asleep, they didn't know what was happening. If things worked as planned, they would be spreading the peanut butter from their hands onto their faces, their hair—wherever they touched. And right about then, three of the girls would realize there was something in their sleeping bag.

We stopped clanging the bell. We were all giggling and trying to stay quiet.

"Now, when they try to get up, they'll pop the

water balloons," I whispered. "And those whipped cream cans—"

"Poof!" Bethanie said, giggling. "Major explosion."

Gabby cackled. "And then the Jell-O will dye their skin a lovely shade of blue!"

Just then—as in perfect timing!—we heard shrieking. Campers from other cabins had already come outside wondering why the bell was ringing; it was still dark out.

The Monarchs had hurriedly put on their shoes—crushing the eggs inside them and getting their feet totally yolked. Then they ran out of their cabin and stop dead in their tracks, staring at us. We were rolling with laughter. We could tell by the surprised looks on their faces that they weren't expecting us to own up to any of this.

But we did. We wanted credit for the Best. Prank. Ever.

So the Painted Ladies, the calmest cabin around (I almost forgot they were even there), won the secret trip with one of the boys' cabins. I don't care, though. We might not have won the most merit points, but we definitely had more fun. Besides, the field trip is kayaking down the river. And really, I prefer to stay away from anything that even resembles a canoe.

THE DANCE

The counselors and CITs transformed the dining hall into a really cool room with helium balloons and twinkling lights. They even had a DJ.

When a slow song came on, Nona and I went to one side of the room to sit down and take a breather. That lasted for a whole five seconds. Simon, this one geeky guy, came up to us.

Before I had time to think about the fact that Nona just got asked to dance, Jackson was standing in front of me, looking down at his feet, with his hands in his pockets.

"Do you, um . . . want to dance?"

ME? A boy asked ME to dance! Of course I said yes.

AND THE REST IS HISTORY. . . .

Oh, you want to know more, huh? Well, Jackson said he really liked me and gave me his phone number so we can text when camp is over. He said he's liked me ever since that embarrassing day because I was so funny!

Hee hee!
Well, I
try!!

And then he said, "I'm a blogger at my school too."

Have I ever mentioned how quickly rumors can spread? Yeah, so can secrets. How did he find out I write a blog?

Our last night at camp, we were given an extended curfew. So after the dance, we had a goodbye campfire. I'm not sure what I was expecting, but it definitely wasn't sadness.

I mean, there we were, sitting around the campfire with everyone holding hands. We sang some cheesy camp songs, but it was fun. And then everyone promised to return next year. And that's when I got all choked up. Because really? I wasn't ready to leave the next day.

GOODBYE, CRACK-A-TOE!

So summer camp was nothing at all like I expected. I'm sure if my parents knew they were sending me somewhere with Bigfoots (or is it Bigfeet?), rabid stray cats, flaming marshmallows, and food fights, they would've thought twice. But I'm glad they made me come, because my summer was much more interesting and fun than it would have been back home. And I didn't even try to be fancy (in fact, I forgot I was supposed to be doing that about halfway through camp), but I still made a lot of new friends. Not to mention I had the most awesomest cabin. Ever!

I'm still kind of wondering how Jackson found out I'm a blogger.

Each of the girls in the Gray Hairstreaks cabin put one of their trunk decals on my trunk. So now I have something to remember everyone by. And my trunk is super-cute. Bonus!

We all leave camp around the same time, but not everyone's parents are on time picking us up. Dad isn't.

Olivia quickly walks over and hands me a folded-up note before she leaves, which I shove into my pocket. It's probably one of her drawings.

After we hike down the hill to wait for our parents, Jackson comes up to me. I figure I should ask him about the blog so I can know for sure. But it has to be away from everyone else so nobody will overhear. We sit down behind a tree while Nona stays with our luggage.

And then, right when I'm going to ask him about his blog, he kisses me!

I, Sofia Becker, have actually been kissed! I

think I see fireworks and pixie dust and other magical things.

If I were a snowman, I would totally melt.

DAD'S HERE!

I'm still so completely stunned I can barely speak. I can't wait to tell Nona what just happened. I have a feeling she knows something is up, though, because I'm walking around with a perma grin and she keeps looking at me, saying, "What?"

When Dad pulls up, I realize it's actually Mom when she gets out of the car. She races up to us and throws her arms around me and Nona. I guess I missed her as much as she missed me.

"Where's Halli?" I ask.

"She's at home with your dad. I couldn't wait to see you girls!" Then she looks down at our muddy sneakers. "Please clean your shoes off before getting in the car," Mom, aka Mrs. Spotless, says.

Nona takes that as an excuse to just remove her shoes.

I reach down and pluck a leaf sticking to the side of my shoe just as Mom screams:

"DON'T TOUCH THAT!"

"That leaf is poison oak!" she shouts.

I drop it as if it's a marshmallow on fire.

"Oh, no! Now you have to wash your hands. And put your shoes in plastic bags. Does anyone have gloves? And don't touch anything, and I mean ANYTHING, until you get home and take a HOT shower."

She won't even listen to me as I try to explain

to her that I think I might be immune to this poison stuff.

Did I MENTION I get the DRAMATIC part of my personality from my MOM?

"Oh, and look at what I picked up at the camp shop for your sister!" Mom holds up a onesie that says "Krakatow" on the front. Who knows, maybe Halli will come here someday.

"What was that note Olivia gave you?" Nona asks.

I pull the note out of my pocket and unfold the paper.

And she didn't even say anything to anyone. Maybe she's not so bad after all.

"What was your favorite part of camp, girls?" Mom asks.

Nona and I look at each other. Where do we even start?

GREETINGS FROM...
CAMP KRAKATOW

ABOUT THE AUTHOR

Did you hear that Rose Cooper's first boo
Gossip from the Girls' Room, was describe
as "humorous," "bubbly," and "wonderful
entertaining" and as perfect for fans of th
Diary of a Wimpy Kid and *Dork Diaries* series
A self-taught artist, Rose has shown her artwor
in galleries and at art fairs and festival
Writing for children gives her the perfe
excuse to keep in touch with her inner child an
never grow up. She lives in Sacramento, Californi
with her husband, Carl, and their three boy
You can visit Rose's website at rose-cooper.co